The Shock of Love

David Appelbaum

The Shock of Love

ISBN 13: 978-0-9846392-3-6

Library of Congress Control Number: 2011926610

Cover design by Jim Sarfati and All Things That Matter Press
Published in 2011 by All Things That Matter Press

Acknowledgments

The text evolved out of conversations with Christopher Bamford. Inspiration by Kate Hamilton. Images adapted from the *Rosarium Philosophicum* by James Sarfati.

PREFACE

In the eleventh century, Ibn 'Arabi wrote that the world is composed of found manuscripts. The Tibetans call them 'hidden treasure.' As they were located, he went on to say, new facts come to light. The sun rises, civilization flourishes, nature is cultivated, the heart of hearts approaches. Slowly, as we decode them, intelligence grows to meet the truth and hope is born. There is beauty to see. May what I am about to pass on to you be an additional cipher on the way of bringing you the blessed state. I am sure Ibn 'Arabi would agree. He would know straight off that this book is about love and read it with delight. As to judging its worth, he would demur, saying as the poets say, things of love go by no common measure. The circumstances under which it came into my possession, too, would perk his interest. Fact is stranger than fiction and fiction is good when it sticks to facts. Both flourish when there is a hidden intrigue, an adventure behind it all. They make us race along until we get to the end, whether the matter is resolved or not. The very idea of a found book is like that. It reminds us of our human lust for truth. Found books make us want to decipher their meaning, for it is never apparent or obvious what they are about. So it is with *The Shock of Love.*

Each found manuscript lightens the world the way renewed interest lightens the spirit. We are filled with the gods. Each thing, under new light, is born anew. The same birth interested Ibn 'Arabi in his quest for immortality. That supernal light seemed to be there in the manuscript I found. But I did not see it right away. Partly, I reacted negatively to the poem that lay on top of the folder. Why it happened in this way I cannot say since to this day it sticks in my mind. It goes:

This is a book of truth,
of love, of heart,
a book that remembers.
It will be held in the hands of a will that reads
forging it
in the act of reading itself.

David Appelbaum

It is for the heart
to remember to read
the ever-present, ever-loving
book that is open long before
I open now to write
to you, my beloved,
whose identity
is yet unknown.

Precious in sentiment, the poem seemed to lay in ambush of me. I believe now it was partly intentional that it was there first. Whether Paolo meant it that way cannot be known, but the manuscript had a secret alliance with the poem, like a prologue to a text. The verse alludes to a path of transformation older than Ibn 'Arabi. Its author obviously was familiar with hermetic ideas of scribes who worked during a late Neolithic age.If one believes Plato, scribes then possessed sacred knowledge since lost — due to the profanation of the act of writing. Their priestly work was designed to invoke a special memory of the ever-present source of truth and love. Once sounded, the invocation allowed them, through writing, to move toward the source of truth as their destiny. Their invocation, as much as has come down in history, involves a solemn celebration of transcendent love. Love was the preoccupation of an ancient scribe to whom letter, word, and tongue were still sacred. The function of writing was simple. Scribes built *vessels of the transcendent*, always on the lookout for new forms in which to hold the ungraspable. Their recorded transcriptions lay 'in their hearts,' to which they gave a precise meaning. This, as far as we can determine, is that the heart is an inner dwelling where one feels love of self. When this reality is kept in mind, writing seeks to open the heart to an acceptance of things. The inscription of early days was as always performed in the language of love. For love is what the scribes of Hermes mean to remember. When a book is not a vessel, it is profane and blasphemous, and a reader of the work would remain an outcast to love's service.

Paolo's poem was a fortuitous find, the key to a treasure chest. The manuscript itself echoed the plan prefigured in the poem. It was not difficult to notice its outward organization was echoed in themes having a neo-Platonic flavor. More specifically, I heard the voice of Apuleis, who wrote during early Christian times. He is best known today for *The Golden Ass*, a novel in which he devised narratives of love that endure to this day. It is here that we find for the first time the story of Psyche and Eros, in which Soul must undergo a number of arduous tests to regain her beloved Eros or Love. The book itself is a work that demonstrates how writing functions as a vessel. A reader feels how love invites desire to become more refined and love more fittingly beloved. At each stage, the reader shares the taste of immortality that desire can grant. Of course Apuleis is a late master of the art. The adventure—and root discovery— of the transformative power of desire dates back to Orphism, a school of esoteric knowledge, whose beginnings are timeless. The poem, too, has keynotes of Orpheus, but this is jumping ahead. I did not know nearly this much on first reading. What I felt was that I was in contact with an undated history that belonged to an era when the needs of human and divine love were better understood.

On first reading, too, the manuscript had the labyrinthine quality of an extended meditative fantasy. This kind of device is essentially a map of the imagination that enters the depths of the self. As I reread it, I found it deeply inventive, to the degree that the reader's imaginative capacities are quickened. Since transcendental imagination, as Ibn's practitioners' knew, has the capacity to heal self-loathing and open the soul to an experience of love directly. In the proper hands, it can work a cure to our mortal sin of fragmentation. There are many historical examples of such meditations and some are accompanied by drawings, which are meant to suggest a correspondence of image and word. This manuscript also employed illustrations. Usually the approach is selective and eclectic, not belonging to one school of another, but obeying certain practical necessities, known only to the author. Sometimes, intentional errors, distortions, or mis-numbered pages were included. Paolo's manuscript seemed to abound in themes and methodologies arbitrarily chosen and even encrypted, and even on further study I doubted that they possessed their own integrity. As other workers found, the imaginative faculty is fundamentally alchemical in its reasoning. Perhaps when fully deciphered, Paolo's would offer a complex set of directions for a single recipe. In any event, what is 'cooked' are the reader's desires and the gold of the process is none other than immortality. I, the reader, quickly found myself in the alchemist's flask, undergoing 'distillation.'

I will say enough to say the book casts a strange spell. Paolo's use of language, with its slight archaism, is deceptively abstract. Speaking of things long forgotten, it seems distant and dispassionate, but its effect is the opposite. The words warm the chill of existence. At the same time, when read with care, the document gives its own rules for reading. I wish early on that they had come clearer to me. There was the obvious importance of moving slowly enough to let the words sink in. My reading habits were challenged. Impatience and speed were obstacles. Slowly, and feeling myself a backward pupil, I learned to adapt. A simple doggedness led me to the key of the whole puzzle. With it in hand, I feel confident that Paolo's work was meant to be shared and that sharing the manuscript will ease me of my burden of obligation.

There is one early suspicion I ought to mention. Even before finishing, I felt the book had a dark origin. To my mind, it had 'been written.' I mean it seems a specimen of automatic writing. The hand that transcribed it is different from the voice that spoke it inwardly. Its source is apparently other than the author's life experience. Like a narration of an altered state, it calls to mind Plato's image of a spirit life that flits between the divine and the human. Plato tells how it is responsible for prophecy and enchantment and many other unworldly things. The manuscript had that aura. It also reminded me of the eerie events that surrounded Yeats on his honeymoon when he discovered his newlywed bride spoke 'with tongues' in her sleep. Copying her words, he composed poetry, adding little or nothing to the transcription. In the case of Paolo's work, the suspicion was fueled by my recognition that the voice of its alleged author did not belong to my former colleague in whose handwriting it was written. Besides, the briefest textual analysis reveals archaisms and vernacular, consistent throughout, that suggest the thought had no place in the rest of his large corpus. Nothing in the man's academic or public commitments can account for the singular intention of this work: to transform through love. In that regard, I would add only that it was strong and effective.

Which brings me to a second possibility. If I discount the notion, which may be insane, that he channeled it, then was it an act of recollection—of a life hidden in all intents and purposes from our eyes? Where else could he have found the wherewithal to forge a will to love? A curious blend of intrigue is at work. Did the story of the manuscript grow out of the work or the other way around? Text and context: they are caduceus-like, the two snakes mating with some deep passion. That, in itself, seems incongruous. Paolo, as I knew him, was a drab and colorless personality, with little flare to his professional life. Had he hidden his passion? He never went out or took part in the petty social life of the valley. Though he liked classical guitar, he did not enjoy good food, drink, or, apparently, women. He was no nature lover either though he took long, solitary bike rides. If he had a passionate interest, he kept it private, even to his few associates like myself. Outwardly, he seemed a man who used up his vitality earlier and then succumbed to a tedium. His eyes expressed it and it was accentuated by his dishevelment that worsened in later years. At the time of his disappearance, he was a known 'minimalist' in his approach to campus activities. He did only what he had to: classes, meetings with students during office hours, but never lunch with colleagues or faculty meetings. What in his inner life was the authentic attitude, whether discouragement, spiritual decrepitude, or an other-worldly yearning was hard to say. There were not many who would have bothered to speculate on the causes of Paolo's isolation other than that they were chronic and hopeless. These were some outer circumstances surrounding my discover of the manuscript. You can begin to imagine my great astonishment. The book Paola had written was a book of love. It opened like a purloined love-letter. I became a reader.

Had I been blind to the fact that Paolo was a lover, if only in the abstract? Not entirely, since his world-weariness felt like the attitude of some wounded soldier of love. The book attested to his grasp of an arcane theory. It had overtones of the style of the hermeticism of the high Renaissance, when culture was bent on unearthing the philosopher's stone which could turn desire into love. What if it were only an academic exercise, a pavlovian reflex left over from dead intellectual pursuits? Or had his life driven him to write a book on the most intensely personal subject under the sun. Questions swarmed around me as I read. Seen in retrospect, my blindness of this project of his had to do with the environment.The state college where we worked is a gray and nondescript complex of buildings set in a large river valley. Intelligent souls get easily lost there and give up their aims in favor of mere survival in a comfortable existence, far from centers of cultural conflict. They turn from the challenge of creativity, languish, and become dead wood. The college provides a perfect camouflage. No one has to conceal a real character because no one looks for one. The job is already done. So it was unlikely for anyone to look for a devotee to love's secrets to live in the desert. Paolo could conduct his experiments without attracting notice. *The Shock of Love* is a journal of his laboratory. As probably, it is the record of a spy in the house of love as he gathers intelligence on the real design of nature.

Let me go back a few steps. From his dossier, Paolo was professor and member of the Department of Romance Languages. Though he once joked about being a direct descendent of Benvenuto Cellini, the incomparable Renaissance goldsmith and sculptor, Paolo was from peasant stock. As a young man, he may have imitated his namesake's flamboyance. But as he progressed, he turned out to be more of a technician trained in grammar, semiotics, and more comfortable with noun clauses than with romance. He favored the endings of different declensions over the heroic endings of troubadour stories. Graduate study had washed him almost clean of the ethnic characteristics of his forebears. He didn't gesture with his hands, nor did he speak with energy and expression.

Although he had become a 'white' Italian, he was also a lapsed Catholic. That was a source of guilt and rebellion that colored his deepest decisions. I have to recreate his youthful ambitions through an act of imagination. By the time I arrived in the valley, Paolo had already begun to go to seed. Even then, he wouldn't shave for a week and wore the same rumpled blue suit. This was barely after the time when people awaited the maturation of great promise. He was still recognized as the golden boy of the Department who had been hired fresh out of Yale. He emanated great knowledge of all aspects of late medieval and early renaissance literature, especially those that focused on love. The chair of his thesis committee wrote that Paolo's analysis of Cavalcanti's 'poetry of bodily contradiction' could be expected to set a new standard of research into Dante's circle of friends. That sounds ironic. Could the members have foreseen Paolo's work degenerating into a set of dog-eared lecture notes? I doubt it. When he was fresh from graduate school, students flocked to his classes, just to witness the phenomenon. Inspirational, articulate, and clear were their enthusiastic descriptions of his words. In those days, we were not surprised to see a young student wandering around campus dazed, reading a copy of the Troubadours or the *Divine Comedy* for Paolo's class.

The young Paolo was a man of bright intensity who flashed a grin I can see now in the photos that lined his office. They outlined a history to the casual viewer: Paolo on visits to museums in Florence, sabbatical in the Tuscan Alps, barbecuing seafood in his backyard, holding a child I saw on campus as a freshman. And as for his young wife, Felicia, I imagine his reciting long passages of *Vita nuova* in beautiful old Italian or hand-copying a Guido Cavalcanti sonnet on parchment. In the faded picture, his were eyes of love, looking toward her. In those early days, he wasn't at all flightiness about his career. Students of his took trips to Rome or Milan or Venice. The best had a study year abroad in his program in Naples. He gave himself to it from a sense of joy, to teach Renaissance love literature. Then Felicia took her own life.

It is strange how little I know about the time before his wife's suicide. To this day, the circumstances remain obscure. Immediately after her death, everything was different. His annual faculty report stopped giving accounts of foreign study, work with the Italian Club, or research at Columbia University's *Casa Italiana*. In retrospect, many of us must have viewed her passing through rose-colored glasses. Paolo was careful to screen his own feelings. For me, there was a part that believed she was always pushing him to achieve. Her death was a relief for me, and, I thought, liberation for him. The sad truth is, it was nothing of the sort. He no longer hungered for professional recognition and drew a cloak of anonymity tightly around his affairs. To all intents and purposes, Paolo vanished.

There is a need for confidence in matters of intimacy, and all love is one. As do many students of love, Paolo left a letter and a diary. I have no plan to divulge the substance of either, but certain things can be safely said. The letter makes clear that I am his literary executor, which imposes its own obligations. But there is the demand of truth. Nonetheless, it is important to know what Paolo wrote in his journal the day of his wife's death. It is a small, square book, covered in fine Corsican leather, and for some reason I imagine his delicate hand passing over the page with the pen's barrel warmed by his fingers that day of great mourning. On 2 October, he wrote, 'She was my rose. Now she is gone. I, like Dante, like Orpheus, will have to seek her in the other world.' For two whole years, there is no entry. Then when he takes the record up again, his hand-writing has changed. It has lost its grace and become dark and heavy. The language, too, grows more cloaked, inflected with symbolism. There are numerous references to his heroes, Dante and before him, Orpheus. He writes of their mission and how they tell no one when they leave in its pursuit. They pick up one day to find their beloved in the fields of death. He refers to an Eastern Orthodox retreat center and his conversations there with a monk. The diary intimates strongly how Paolo must have cast his lot with both groups and in their shared interest in the after-death state. There are continual references to myths and accounts of ancient practices concerning death. He details an enigmatic descent into a land where nothing lives and where a reunion with the loved one is possible. He describes tests, trials, struggles against obstacles of the deep. In that, he grasps for a way of thinking that is against nature. He questions what it takes to make the crossing.

The whole thing must have occupied him to the point of an obsession. The outward semblance of a life really signified his disappearance to the world. During this period, the diary chronicles his relationship with a strange group in France. It tells how it is forbidden to him to reveal its activities, but it clearly becomes a prime concern. At least, this is how I see it. Then, it comes to an end. What happened actually is unknown. To this day, there is a missing person report filed with the local State Department office. Their investigators state that he died, though no body has ever been recovered. There are accounts of death on a deserted Italian highway in a collision with a drunk driver, or alternatively of a drowning in the Adriatic, near the island of Lesbos. Around the campus, there are rumors of a shadowy life and a sordid real estate deal since Paolo had some skeletons in the closet. But this is so much humming in the wind. Italy was coming home to Paolo. I do not think he perished there, though he wanted it to look like that. It was a death of another sort. He felt he had to be true to what he had written in *The Shock of Love*. He had drawn up the specifications of an encounter with death, and he had to live by his words.

Love and death form the deepest philosophical opposition. We need only to return to the roots of our thinking to find it. Diotima, Socrates' incomparable teacher, pictures life in a continual struggle with death as it seduces aggression in order to clear the way for a sense of immortality. Plato, Socrates' devoted student, writes of consciousness in that way. Consciousness is nothing other than love's battle with domination by death. It works itself out in the dialectical ascent to a timeless reality. Let us not forget that Paolo was at heart a Platonic Italian or Sicilian Platonist. Much was at stake in his search for his beloved—not in the least the destiny of his own philosophical heritage. In a sabbatical year conversation, he once said, 'Love cannot die. It simply needs the proper food to sustain it through eternity.' His research lay there. I take his disappearance to serve notice to our death-bound civilization that he found himself beyond a life-or-death struggle, and that now a kind of immortal life was his.

It took several months in the College library to get a grasp on the manuscript. First, I reread Paolo's annual lecture to the Italian Club, entitled 'Love Undying,' in which he discusses early Greek myths that played into Renaissance texts on incorruptible love. Then, after Plato, I scoured Hesiod, Empedocles, Aristotle, and the Stoics. I looked into Plotinus and Augustine, to see how classical thought became infected with Christian. I devoured the works of Pico della Mirandola, with its heady dash of hermetic obscurity. And of course, more and more Dante and the schools he had visited. But Paolo is not an obvious soul and nothing in his approach is obvious. Maybe no obvious approach exists. The after-death state is an enigma, or the stuff of enigma itself. Facts are few, the prized gems of ancient schools most of which have been lost. A few suggestive illustrations in a book or two, but not much more. Whether this made it easier for Paolo's own peculiar genius is difficult to say. It is ambiguous how much is his and how much he borrowed. Then again, if the whole thing is the result of a dark voice at midnight, his book raises even deeper questions.

To call the project a book of love makes it a peculiar book or about a peculiar love. It is both—a love book for a dead soul, for whom the book brings new life. That, I take it, is the purpose behind Dante's *Nuova vita*. It purges the memory by glaring confession and permits real love to write itself indelibly on the inner being. A soul is reborn as that which is written there. Many religions pray for the souls of the dead and deceased. Paolo's book offers a different prayer. It prays for the soul of the living dead. The prayer is for rebirth of a feeling of immortality that is inborn to each person. Both prayers uplift the hearer, but one is to lift the grief for another, and the second, grief for oneself. Whenever that despair dissipates, according to the Desert Fathers, we feel our immortal selves. Like some Renaissance explorer, was Paolo after the fountain of immortality, from whose brim falls the waters of immortality? I assume his book opened the door to an ever-renewing life and he is there now. From this, it follows that there must have been a second woman, a woman 'distilled' by alchemy.

Alchemy was a strange science even in Renaissance times. It is stranger now, and stranger since it has all but disappeared. As intellectual curiosity stirred in the late Medieval times, it had to be called back from nonexistence by an avid interest in Egyptian esoterics. Greater anticipation awaited Ficino's translations of the works of Hermes Trismegistus than those of Plato. Thrice-born Hermes, master of the after-death state. To Ficino's mind, both were guidebooks to the land of the dead. Both contained 'recipes' of incorruptibility. They clarified where myth had been vague regarding the hope to enter the other region while still alive. Hermes is the infallible guide. To what process? That refining a raw material. The end-result is more valuable, less perishable, and subject to fewer external forces. It becomes a substance unto itself, a stone. The aim of Hermes' alchemy is to conjure a product immune to degeneration. Did Paolo succeed? A certain degree of success would seem the entry-fee for writing an alchemical book of love.

Do not think it is a mere stylistic choice of Paolo's, to write a post-modern text of hermetic alchemy. True, he learned the tricks of the Italian poets from his graduate studies. From there and early Catholic schooling, he had access to clues about what Dante was doing. *Vita nuova* did not discover the key to transformation but impeccably employed it. To take his own heart as a book, Dante can inscribe the story of his now departed beloved. Dante writes:

> *These thoughts of mine and sighs which forth I send*
> *Within my heart to sharper anguish grow,*
> *Where Love in mortal pallor lies in pain;*
> *For in the deep recesses of their woe*
> *The sweet name of my Lady they have penned*
> *And many words to tell her death again.*

Dante does not, however, reveal he also holds the power to revise her story and in the revision, to bring her life again. The crux lies in transforming himself and the knowledge gained of living and dying. I think of Paolo's work in a similar vein. Like Dante, he writes a memory book with a specific program. This is no modern memoir that serves a history up to the reader. Its sights are on *re-cording*, a word which turns back to the Latin word for *heart, cordis*. In writing, Paola found a way to make a heart incorruptible. With it, he could safely visit the land of the dead, and safely return. In its crucible, he distilled sentiments and thoughts regarding his dead wife and write them into an indelible ink of the incorruptible word. With his map of the underworld, he produced a text of our time to help guide him to his beloved. But note. The book is indiscriminate with respect to its reader. It can guide anyone who wishes to be led.

Even here, I acknowledge a curious ambiguity in the project. Was his book to lead him to the land of the dead, or to his own heart? Or was his heart that wasteland, parched for words of immortal love? An image of Paolo's wane face returns the day he delivered the eulogy at his department chair's memorial service. He said, 'To understand a person, one must look past his mortality, to a part immune to the changing face of life.' I had assumed he was wasting away from a loveless life, but what if it were the opposite—burning up in the intensity of his search for love? Could the Great Work have been sucking the animal life from poor Paolo as he tended, night after night, the intense flame of his furnace? Which provokes another question: Was he a hapless apostle of that craze of the Renaissance, to transmute crude ore into gold, that produces only fits of psychopathology? Even as I ask it, I have to confess an ignorance. A real answer would come from reading *The Shock of Love* and following its guidance.

I nonetheless want to hazard a conjecture. The result cannot be fame or wealth or recognition. Paolo's withdrawal from the academic grove was a rejection of those values. One can imagine that the curtain he drew permitted him to become part of the book. The work demanded no less. One immediate result was to intensify the hiding itself. Only in solitude could he exchange, as the Lord did for Ezekiel, his dead heart of stone for one of flesh. To say he died to his old life is not accurate since the reverse is what happened. I am not talking only of my hypothesis. A year before his disappearance, there is an exclamatory entry in his diary. It goes: 'I have found her! In the least expected, but most expected place, there she was, having coffee in a sidewalk café!' The time coincides with the penultimate trip he took to Tuscany. It was a two-week jaunt, about which he said to me, 'If I don't get away from here, I'll crack up.' I infer it was a second turning point that had an intimate connection with his written work. In retrospect, he spent his last year at the College making preparations for the final rendezvous that this meeting prefigured.

What about his life? Was its visible course as poetic and ironic as it appeared? What is the meaning of irony? A vital young man is washed to the shore of a deserted beach of intellectual life. He then proceeds to waste away until a tragic death on holiday provides the closing line. That is the story in the local paper and faculty dining room. The Italian police say he went swimming alone in a deep island cove with dangerous riptides. The Department of Romance Language held a memorial service the next month. It was surprisingly well attended, at least for one had all but burned his bridges behind him. A modest scholarship for graduate study was established in his name by the Alumni Association. They decided to offer Guthrie's study on the Orphic religion to the first winner. Other small reminders of the life emerged—his work for homeless children, his dedication to a sick cousin in Florida, his active correspondence is government officials on the subject of abortion—but none do justice to the man. For that, there is the manuscript.

I haven't tinkered much with the account Paolo wanted believed. It's obvious that he expected his work to be found—clues like the letter to the president of the College, his papers left in a tidy bundle, an empty post-office box, a dead parrot. He wanted it discovered at the right time, one that did not blow his cover. That was the rhapsodic soul of an Italian alchemist. I can almost see the corners of his mouth curl in a sardonic smile. 'Professor on leave disappears at Italian sea resort and is mourned by colleagues and students.' The headline is incongruously sentimental. Paolo never was, not about his wife's tragic suicide, nor about the intention subsequent to it. His disappearance is just another 'act' in his book of memory, his love-book. It was the book's most brilliant inscription. By its stroke, he exchanged his life in the Department of Romance Languages for words of love in his heart. Wasn't this what he had been seeking? It was its own kind of immortality.

It was Horace, in an ode, who writes,

> *Some part of me will live and not be given*
> *Over into the hands of the death goddess.*

Paolo may have felt similar when he, a master-scribe, enfolded his life to a book of love. It was not merely a literary way, but a literal one, to beat death. I almost wrote, cheat death, but that's another matter. Cheating wasn't the thought of the Renaissance artisans who rediscovered the work of antiquity, which, by a secret process, could produce an undying state. In the alchemy of writing, the point is for the author to turn himself into a character who writes the book of the author's memory. In this way, he is 'cooked' in the process of embodying the writer's character and inherits the philosopher's stone. He becomes words remembered by heart and lives their life—a life renewed by each reader. Perhaps Horace meant this. If not, it is, in my own simple way of understanding Paolo's accomplishment. After all, his deep fascination with dust-covered books was not simply to stare at their arcane line drawings. When writing an alchemical text, the writer seeks contact with a source of transmutation. When the magical force is present, the crude lead of the literal mind turns into the gold of imagination. Passed from one soul to the next, its truth, as Plato wrote, kindles a blaze of love in another's heart. This image may contain the essence of immortality. In any event, those touched are in a state that is ever-fresh, ever-new. If this is Horace's allusion, then he knew the path which is Orphic. Perhaps we can add his smile to Ibn 'Arabi's and to Paolo's. I feel he beat death at its own game and would add my word's testimony to the list. Perhaps it likewise testifies to Paolo's success in that field.

Perhaps you, the reader, can see how his work exerts an influence on me. It has bade me come out of my dream and take a serious look at what Paolo was concerned about. It even invites me to join his endeavor, to elaborate on his text of love, both for my sake and that of the subject. To be more forthright, I find it constantly affects my mind with figures of its themes—the fool, the stranger, the guide, and Orpheus himself—and has subtly converted me to its way of thinking. If not conversion, it is a strength of persuasion that is rare. It is that which impels me to take the bold step of seeking its publication. Is it strange that I, who never considered love's transformation, am now asked to be its emissary to the world? Paolo showed me rationality is secondary once you have taken a step on the solitary inward journey. He has led me to the enigmatic place beyond places—the 'land of the dead,' without location or life, null-point of the universe, an omnipresent absurdity. I followed his directions and was affected. Although I cannot say, as with love, the change was complete and for the better.

The chief reason to doubt stories of Paolo's demise lies there. He uncovered the secret to an enduring life and an accidental ending is too simplistic. Why not picture him with his new love, found the summer before he vanished? Right now, see him in Florence, Venice, or Tuscany, leading the cultured life one dreams of in this prim bourgeois valley. That is the ending to the drama that I would write. Does love pride itself in rescuing you after a long drought, as it did Goethe in his *Roman Elegies*? Besides, Paolo may be working on his text, refining and editing, or he may be now on a second volume. This is pure conjecture. Paolo may be in a more remote place, in South America, or really dead. If he is really gone, I hope it was from 'experimentation' and not lassitude of soul that gave its last breath up easily. It would disappoint me if he succumbed without a fight.

This said, I present *The Shock of Love* to you. I have already given some understanding of the work and its author, as well as my reasons for having it published. Do not in this context think of me as reporting his work, like a reviewer who gives an *explication de texte*. I cannot conceive of having such an alienated relation to the material. I am not offering a critique or exegesis, and could not, not after reading. I am a reader and want to be for as long as the binding holds the pages of the book together. The comparison may not be totally mad, but Solomon wished for a listening heart. My wish is like that, for engagement, not distance. Does not the reader want to inscribe the heart with the text of love until it is perfectly legible? With that done, each and every act will be consecrated by a reading in it. This is a lofty thought and I am very far from that, too often foolishly forgetful. In the din of the world, reading's demands of delicacy and care are often beyond me. Yet when I pick up the book of Paolo's again, I see the absolute necessity of it. Does that make me a student in his class? What does that make him? A seer, saint, or syncreticist? A genius, by all accounts.

A large claim and I make it with trepidation. It interests me that the Paolo I knew as a young intellectual was no genius. Bright, ambitious, energetic, he was on track to achieve a far more limited end. Genius was something he grew into. This adds greatly to the text's intrigue. That he is its author in spite of how ill-suited he was to the task suggests another force at work. I respect him the more for his involvement with it, whatever name we give. *Desire*, Paolo liked to write, is a word that comes from the stars, *sideris* in Latin. This is an echo of the divine Plato's school that desire originates in heaven and is brought to earth by 'messengers' like love. May it be that desire transformed me, through its close reading of what I hadn't then uncovered in my own heart. For that is my strong impression of what was at work with Paolo. That is to admit happily that his genius may bring a great hope. In its wake, the book beckons to be opened and to allow us, its readers, to be smitten by what we find there in our hearts.

The Shock of Love

By

Paolo Cellini

A FOREWORD BY THE AUTHOR

What is a 'book of the heart' if not a living question? For a self that lacks nothing is forever questioning a self that is constantly lacking. The book triumphs over a weak memory so that its author might remember its real identity. This kind of book, I suspect, was once more common. In bygone days, such books served as guides. Because I am credulous, the book I am writing opens the heart by making it known. I therefore feel compelled to write, though in question. Is the book writing itself, or is it being written? Ambivalence prevents my saying which, and not just the fact that the first is still being confirmed. That comes as a confession. As I write, I have not yet read the book but plan to as soon as I finish.

Beginning with a confession places me in a strange position—one related to the ignorance in you, the reader. You do not know what to expect, either. We are equals with respect to the equation of reading with writing. The ancient scribes were first to use writing as a confessional. They read the book they had written to know the heart on which they had just inscribed. That heart was the same that belonged to the self. All writers confess in the same mode, the mode of self-confession. They confess a felt lack of purity and use the book to transform crude, 'sinful' material into a metal whose virtue is gold. The end-product I allude to goes by many names and is the Name itself, the philosophers' stone, truth, the incorruptible consciousness. It takes the form of a book. Confession keeps the word true to the extent the heart carries it in love. Confession reveals that love is the heart-word, written over and again, as the heart lives on. My confession to you, the reader, is how a book of love serves a sacred function. The force of reconciliation, whose source is the heart, will subsequently direct the task to the reader. You may read its pages with knowing eyes. There, thought born from the pen finds its way to impregnate the heart. The embryo in the heart's fertile womb contains the secret identity—whose birth fulfills the sole responsibility of authorship. The heart sick with 'hope deferred' needs love and desire. Otherwise, it will dry up, and life wither in the arid desert. Readers must forgive my weakness for matters of conscience.

David Appelbaum

It is so. All matters of conscience have one end: to see to it that the intellect remember what takes precedence. They also ordain that an undertaking of this kind make explicit reference to the principle upon beginning. This is that prayer, to which you, the reader, bear witness. So mote it be.

LOVE'S FOOL

I will speak of love and desire. In my discourse, the fool begins. The fool is not an image of love, but holds the place for it. For that reason, the fool is universally loved, and what we love, we become. The first challenge of a book of love is to recognize the fool, the nearest and dearest to a beloved. The challenge is both simplest and most difficult since whoever has fallen in love is foolish. To speak of the fool is to speak most personally and openly—of ourselves. We are love's fool and to know it is the first and last step toward acquiring the gold of self-knowledge.

Who is the fool, the appointed preamble of a treatise on love? The fool awakens to a riddle that flourished in antiquity, and that suffices for a name. The riddle runs: what adds or subtracts nothing to life yet always figures in? A person's reply is a signature. It separates fools from the rest because anyone who explains this 'nothing' belies a dull, and rather unfoolish mind. The fool takes the conundrum to experience, and in particular, the mute melody that constantly accompanies moments of life without in the least interfering. This 'no-thing' is the attention, without which we are lost. Only the attention adds or subtracts nothing at all to the event, and yet contains the whole of it. If love—our search's grail—is to be anywhere felt, it must first calculate the value of life's meaning. This equals the 'zero' of the attention. Mathematically, it follows that the fool, who symbolizes the attention, first brings love to mind, since love is but the attention in its glorified, ecstatic body. Everything else in my treatise relates to the fool. If loveless, there is no relation at all, hence, no hope for the transformation of love's glory. Do not read farther if you have no love for fools. A fool, if true, is worthy if love is to turn impulsive, selfish desire into an ever-renewing source.

You may recall a story in the Upanishads, of two birds in a tree who are 'dear companions.' The first bird eats the sweet fruit while the second only sits and watches. The fool behaves like the second bird. It is removed from life's enjoyments and sufferings but shadows each and every one, the closest of witnesses. The fool, too, is the consummate outsider who has friendships with no one and everyone, and who looks on without judgment, expectation, or disappointment. That acceptance gives supreme evidence of love. That we find love embodied in such an unexpected place makes us perceive differently. When we do, we see how the fool engenders love itself, an impartial love, a love for things as they are—though the fool is no saint. Fool's love is singular in the way that zero is, being no number but an accompaniment to all. Its source is elsewhere. Both zero and the fool serve as conduits of the beyond, its laws, its inscrutability, and its infinite intimacy with our every breath. But while zero is silent, the fool is full of ironic declarations to us, the audience, who are not yet awake to the point of glorification—love.

In the Tarot deck, you will find a truer understanding of the fool's dimwit nullity. The fool's card is numbered '0,' leaving it ambiguous whether it begins or ends the major arcana. Zero means the fool infiltrates situations as cipher. A cipher denotes absence of quantity, emptiness, the setting whose place must remain vacant. The fool relentlessly strives to become the thing ciphered—and succeeds surpassingly. The vacancy has to do with the possessor of the place, for it is held in reserve for no mortal but by the god, love. Does it surprise you to call love divine? That means that the attention is a divine steward, stalwart in place-keeping. The brilliance of the Tarot's fool is that of a keeper, no more, no less. The fool guards a place for love. In the god's absence, the fool weeps, and in the divine presence, washes love's feet with tears of joy. This you must also know. Such a one walks the earth beyond pride and waits for the beloved, who is awaited and with what patience of resolve.

The fool may be dressed in piebald or motley, as harlequin, clown, or court jester, but when love comes, the fool awakens. An astoundingly wide range of feeling flows then, a river. When we are touched, we see the fool in our heart, the heart's fool, an ageless soul with an open wound from which festers life's troubles. Who could have a greater sense of providence and the human place, of humility? Because the heart is worn on the sleeve, the fool speaks truth without meaning to—effortlessly, like a child. Truth brims from a fool's mouth! Just as we marvel at a child's truthfulness and squirm with its revelation, so the fool coincides perfectly with language. The utter congruence dismays us, who know too well the crack through which the lie seeps in. Feeling pours without interruption, whether applauded or threatened with death. There is no stop of it. The fool is a fountain, and its source attentively keeps watch over us in our sleep and sluggishness. Keeper of love's fountain, the fool pities our thirst and would have us drink our draught deeply. It is our paradoxical fate. As the fountain pours its loving waters, the heart is preoccupied and fearful with life. The patient fool's vigil brims with foolish hope that our sleep mix with love's waters. Remember how Lear's fool sings,

> *The man that makes his toe,*
> *What he his heart should make,*
> *Shall of a corn cry woe,*
> *And turn his sleep to wake.*

Turn your thoughts to my science that teaches how to produce gold out of the coarse, ordinary material of life, and ask, where does the fool come in? Since the fool is love's watchword and no god, folly is neither holy nor pious, or by the same token, neither unholy nor impious. The fool waits for the transmutation to begin and, for that reason, is not God's fool, sung by Saint Paul, since the fool who adores and praises nothing still has a transcendent mission. Making gold requires the fool's cooperation, but it is not fool's gold that is produced. How the fool accomplishes this purpose is beyond ciphers and no speech can clarify it. Compare the function to a catalyst in the formula of love's glorified body. Or, to return the trope to deciphering, the fool speaks in riddle and love returns. The fool's tongue is schooled in that oracular, middle-voice word of a truth that lacks enumeration. How the fool lives in constant remembrance of love has to do with the crucible, fire, and patience. His knowledge refers to an original vessel of love. Into it is placed prime matter—impulsive desire—that love feels in its first stirring. This does not mean the fool is constantly in love, though some are like that. But in solitude, the fool passionately suffers the love that is not yet born, for life refuses to be in love's arms. The suffering is of nature, which is about to give birth. Nature suffers desire even though it is natural because it is born unloving. The fool desires love but lacks authority to obtain the object, and so, is forced to wait on the transformation. Folly's patience stems from acquaintance with the internal dynamics of the furnace and its tending. The fool, you could say, is the alchemist—and that is you, the reader, who now oversees the flame, as raw material turns to the gold of pure loving desire.

We know the fool brings laughter. But do we laugh because the fool is constantly the fool? Beyond integrity, the fool heralds all transformation. The quicksilver of attention possesses a quixotic property that surprises, amazes, or dismays us. It, like the fool, survives in the face of loss since we mortals, forever busy as bees to the hive, rarely have time to receive it. The fool, night watchman of love, sister of the attention, wears a tragic smile on painted lips. See how the fool regards death eye to eye, not to defeat it, but to remember incorruptible love. The fool's virtue is to remove the sting of death with a laugh and an awareness of impermanence. To us who are blind to our mortal nature, the fool can appear a simpleton, moron, or imbecile—naïve to a flaw. But *our* unintelligent consideration of consequences alone glimpses its foolish ineffectiveness. We are dumbstruck by a mercurial logic that speaks in the perishability of meaning. What is once given must twice be taken away, and each pratfall reeks with the comedy of that theft. It may be cruel that we laugh at those tears, but recognizing cruelty as such, we grow sweet and compassionate as a fool.

Do you remember Percival, great fool of the Grail story, who knows loss just before his moment of triumph? He is in the cast of the Grail and it is his for the asking. But the glory is not yet his and God's gift, a precarious proposition. In the inner sanctum, having the Fisher King's ear, he is within a hairsbreadth of an astonishing denouement. You must carefully note what takes place at this junction. There and then, his tongue is dumbstruck and he cannot ask the simplest of questions, what ails thee? The halls of gold, their glory of love, vanish before his eyes and so also, the transformation of his naïve desires. Percival must wander lost countless years before finding the secret castle a second time. He then is able. The truth is that he brings what he forgot the first time, the attention—that nullity—and adds it to the vessel. The food is cooked, the King cured, nature restored, and the fool with love's wisdom in addition to its folly presides.

Simple-minded, the fool loves a consciousness of desire and searches for it until death. Between the storms of night and the wiles of men— from mishap to mishap—the fool perseveres with a single will. Once met with consciousness, the fool will not abide in its loss. All methods of repair are apt to be makeshift, hazardous, or nonexistent. That they defy a logic of means and ends lends proof to the fool's access to a higher logic, or none at all. As you know, Cervantes' Don Quixote says, 'God will find a way to fix everything.' Don Quixote speaks with a blend of insouciance and foreknowledge. God's will is on the curriculum of foolery. Quixote is also human and in the human realm. Conscious desire rarely prevails so the fool, wary of the future, suffers from fears and cowardice. They blot out an ingredient that could take transmutation farther. Think of this whenever you take watch over the fire. Think also how at midnight, in a violent storm, far from home with the king, Lear's fool is concerned about creature comforts. Does he not disregard the one needful thing? 'He that has a house to put's head in has a good head-piece.' But 'the son of Man has no place to lay his head.' Such is a fool's life.

Devotion to conscious desire is foolhardy since it inevitably leads to life's hither side. The fool pays for it with salt. The salt wrung from tears that are wept is like the oyster's pearl. Could I speak later of the birth of conscience, that incomparable stone that grows in the body of a lowly sea-being? A fool's conscience, capable of pricking a king's, comes with a heavy price. It is truly a miracle, a product of will and grace. The conscience, as the fool knows, is not entirely a gift from above, an inner God, shrouded in conditions carefully prepared: an ever-renewed willingness to meet the truth of all situations. What I call 'will' involves dropping the mask under which we hide from life. Then, when you look, you behold the innocent, unfeigned face of yours.

Like love, the fool is a double agent. Love is bitter-sweet. Remember Sappho's lines:

With his venom
irresistible
and bittersweet
that loosener
of limbs, Love
reptile-like
strikes me down

Is that not also the taste of conscience, to this science, a precursor to love? In innocence or with irony, the fool calls us to remember our task. There is sweet love, at ecstatic union, and there is lost love that weeps. The fool teaches that impulsive desire is sorrow done up to appear as joy, as Prometheus did with the sacrificial ox in order to fool the gods and goddesses. He teaches how forgetfulness is the shadow of remembrance and evil, the twin of good. The fool is a mortal in search of the god, the mortal who heeds his inner god and has inklings of a secret identity. That inner god seeks to love life in purity and without corruption, that outer God. But the inner god is aware of the mortal's refusal and the cost of conversion. You also need to bear in mind how conscience is sweet to obey and bitter in disobedience. Love would repair the refusal, but only by enduring its pain. Love, too, is bitter in its sweetness.

The fool yearns for self-knowledge but remains in gentle innocence. Love is innocent when concerned with self-centered impulses of desire, its common form. You could say how innocence is transparent until it grows pained, that is, loses itself. The fool's apparent innocence repeatedly tells of the loss, though not in so many words. Irony may be another name for self-knowing. The irony speaks, as lore tells, how love at its heart seeks only to know itself, and the more it seeks, the more it loves the mystery in which it wraps its heart—the riddle, the enigma, the Other. It loves what lives beyond desire's impulsive side and does not submit to quick gratification. It senses what else is sought by an embryonic human soul. The fool is supplied by the irony of change, constant in inconstancy. Desire learns that good fortune is limited, though the task of love is without bounds. In love always, folly is not everywhere smiled upon by luck. When losing in love, the fool finds the bitter of the bittersweet, which is a remorse at forgetting the beloved. The terms of life's bargain with love are made preeminently clear. Take note of what the fool teaches. The payment is to be made with salt. Masters of the Tarot have shown you this fact. On the fool's card, the figure carries a sack of salt over one shoulder, while the fool lurches toward the rim of the abyss.

What is salt and how is it assayed? Salt, mineral of life, of the moon, the sea, night, and a woman's tears, is a complex element. This means it already has evolved from simples. Evolution proceeds through a process of devotion. There is no salt in attending innocence since salt attends the passage to mature being. Salt is the coin of payment when it comes to transformation. Salt refers to the tears of suffering, for that is their taste. With regard to salt, the fool is the awakened one and tears are as much a signature of the fool as foolery. This is why, when we regard rightly, the fool is seen as an advanced human being, knowledgeable about the way. We rarely do so and almost never hear how 'the way begins much farther along than we think.' The fool, love's keeper, keeps what no man or woman can keep, that secret—which is not difficult since no one asks. Almost no one knows love cannot be kept, but Ophelia tells King Lear anyway. At that, Lear, weeps for love lost. Therewith begins his payment, with salt, for his obliviousness. In the hands of his fool, Lear becomes as devout an alchemist as you will be, which is symbolized by how he and his fool exchange roles. The king becomes a fool for love, love's keeper, and learns of its secret way. The more his tears empty the king of him, even unto zero, the more filled from the fountain above he grows. It pours from a source that makes him yearn for a love glorified and incorruptible.

The fool represents great knowledge posed as idiocy. With the look of Lear's fool, folly as midwife escorts her new-born patient laboriously through the underworld, a birth unto light in truth. In the dark womb journey, knowing and being, male and female, become fused. Lear gives birth to a new king, one now guided by strength of conscience. His life has undergone the sulfurous 'heat of love' by which the heavenly mixes with the chthonic, and is transformed. And the fool who has kept a vigil on the birth of love? The fool remains the same. The unwavering attendance does not interact, preach, or detain in any way, but somehow catalyzes a life-change. There is in truth no means of teaching the doctrine since it is too foolish for the incredulous and too obvious to believers. It appears only as the hidden spring of action that has been informed by love. The fool teaches how no one can grasp the lesson except by being remade a fool.

You may recall how the fool came to love from old accounts of love's origin. They tell how love is born from the wind's copulation with mother night. Inseminated, the night of nights bears a marvelous golden egg, as big as the cosmos, from which love hatched. That is what the devotees of Orpheus say. Love, they continue, then brings into being all manner of things, from galaxies to microbes, each with its own specificity. Love continues to favor its maternal side, night, in its attachment to secrecy, darkness, the charm of dreams, and the warmth of the bed. The father's mark, the airy rush of vitality, is then meant for the fool. This becomes evident when we look at the word *fool* since it still contains a trace of its paternity in its root, *to blow*. The fool listeth where it goeth, moving over the face of the world, kicking up its heels, raising a dust and a storm without being blinded. The wind breathes out and in, and as watchmen, our breaths embody the wind's attentiveness, which is the fool's. In a most timeless guise, the fool incarnates spirit, absolute restlessness that breeds new life wherever it moves. Bearing powers of both father and mother, the fool impregnates each and every moment with the urge to presence. We come to patience and acceptance of it through the fool. That is, we are witness to how both joy and suffering arise with coming life.

This is how it is when the fool appears within—when we fool ourselves. Hostility mixes with affection, antipathy with sympathy. You should mark how to glimpse the war of opposites, for it is to see through the eyes of the fool. For the fool sees the relativity of the world *and* sees through it, to the other world. We who deceive ourselves pay the consequences of our ignorance. We lack a taste for our existence and the joy of the ground beneath. Though the fool knows, do not think the fool is above deception. While folly does not lie to itself, it is hardly immune to bending the truth to impart a lesson, or for sheer tomfoolery. Does the fool not know how life persists at the blurred edges? Or honor the ever-changing shape of truthfulness by putting on the cloak of the shape-shifter? If the truth be out, the fool lives for immediacy. There, the horizon of events is all plastic and ambiguity. What is about to happen is a birthing. With but a glance toward the other realm, the fool, though lacking in reflection, sees past the opposites, toward the ecstatic moment when the night and the wind consummated. There, no opposition had yet reared its head. Because the fool does not reflect on events, either before or after, folly makes a perfect mirror. It never loses the attention. Suffering no loss of that, the fool suffers more than we ever can for the absence of love. To repent that absence—here is where I must initiate you into love's fool.

For an inheritance, the fool is given to comprehend all separate phases of love, from infancy to dotage, and that, all at once. Idealist, adventurer, student, and adept, the fool is also the one who cannot get the lesson right and keeps making foolish mistakes. There is perpetual lust in the approach, an enormous hunger that cannot be sated. Even after love, fatigued, the fool suffers desire. It is a desire for tending to life. The Tarot card signifies the ubiquity of the fool's desire in the way it depicts folly as an ageless nomad. Time does not weigh on a fool's mission any more than gratification does on lust's appetite. This is a most hopeful observation. It says how what is at stake in love's transformation is available everywhere, any time. Desire is as free as the air we breathe. Remember how the fool loves to love and will do anything for it, and you will go far in learning.

The identity of love's guardian is obvious, though the guard is unseen. It is the fool because only a fool is at ease with love's vagaries and neither attached, nor indifferent. The fool is at ease because folly is all ease. It is the line of least resistance because being foolish—or being, period—means to abandon all resistance. The fool simply *is*, which is to say, other than a hard, resistant refusal to exist. The fool's mood has melted self-will by its acceptance of hardship. Striving for any worldly or other-worldly goal has evaporated for the fool is constantly at wit's end. Folly never exceeds itself and, moment by moment, bears its measure within. Because of the self-containment, a fool exudes being even when others are uncomfortable about being and want otherwise. Love is kept safe because the fool lacks alternative actions. Foolishness is composed of contraries, aware of themselves, complementing each other in the restless hunger of spirit. That, I remind you, is the ragtag that the fool for love is. Love's fool is spirit.

Exceeding a guard or keeper, the fool is also a servant to love, incapable of any disobedience . . . to love, that is. This is the difficult lesson of fidelity you must grasp in order to be transformed. It is not a simple-minded morality, for folly has no trouble bending the truth to others unmindful of love and its desires. A servant to love also serves desire that comes in all colors and hues. The fool knows impulsive desire's heated drama better than a lover. If the lover would listen to a fool, we would have no tales of broken hearts. No lover would appear foolish, a victim of folly's impulse but who lacks a fool's knowledge of spontaneity. Unlike the fool, the lover has eyes and ears only for the object and gets drunk on it. Fools never drink, nor do they become intoxicated. They are, too, subject to the exigency of love to have occasion for serious drunkenness. The fool is forever barred from inebriation, while inebriation repeatedly dons the fool's disguise. Yet it is true that we can grow intoxicated with foolishness—and do.

A good example is Alcibiades, Socrates' would-be lover in the *Symposium*. He is no fool, but attempts to act the part in his alcoholic exuberance. Though he plays it to the hilt, he fools none of his companions. Proof of this is how he crashes the party to reveal how he was taken in by love's deception, and everyone can see that. It is a case of blatant self-deception. He told himself Socrates was in love with him because he desired to believe it. Alcibiades wises up enough to realize the danger of love: that we kid ourselves about it. This is auto-intoxication, fantasy without attainment. We owe him an important discovery, which you may stumble on in life—that there is plain fool's gold as well as the real stuff, true fool's gold. Just the same, there are crocodile tears as well as ones that are the salt of love's devoutness. The fool stands in contrast to Alcibiades' performance because of an awareness of where salt comes from and what it is good for. That awareness—of love—arises from nowhere if not beyond the realm of relativity. Its vision binds together the opposites and transcends them with its heartfelt openness. Unlike Alcibiades, the fool opens to the force of life as it descends from a source above. It is a wind coming to inseminate the night with love.

Another important matter you may remember is the fool's relation to the marriage of love. Love marries with an eye resolving the conflicts that threaten to tear things apart. The doctor of antiquity, Empedocles, saw it clearly. It is not a marriage love makes once and for all, but one repeatedly undone by refusal. The gyres go back and forth. Love wins, love loses, refusal wins, refusal capitulates. What secret balm does love possess? That we must seek, though we know the one who possesses the secret. We can study the fool's abiding with love, come what may, and if we listen, we can discover the particulars of love's vow. At that, conflict would cease to reign. A new golden age waits to be born through the fool's truth, but we would be hard-pressed to follow. The fool knows truth because folly is immune to it. It lives beyond truth's threshold, on the near side of truth, and even truth does not know of folly. If we followed, we would have to wander in the desert, guided by God's signs. There, the truth waits under the brilliant night's stars. To understand, you would need to look in the direction of the fool's starlit eyes. Love's marriage is an astral affair. The fool is subject only to the laws of the stars and their own illogical wisdom. Look at the Pierrot Makiage and see how the eyes are made up as stars. Is this why we believe that marriages are made in heaven and lovers are star-crossed?

What is love's marriage but a book of love written by a fool. It is a book for changing crude desirousness into love's desire. It is to be read only in starlight, for that is the substance of a fool's wisdom. Under what light are you reading? Love's marriage celebrates the union of Hermes and Aphrodite, the hermetic art with the erotic, mercury with sulfur. This is an exemplary marriage, a combining of opposites. Aphrodite is sexual attractiveness. Hermes guards the path toward being and the transcendental realm. They marry and the fool is full of joy. The fool celebrates their marriage in a capacity other than as a mere celebrant. Strangely, he is a product of the union, the androgynous child, risen to the sphere of the stars, nowhere and everywhere. At once the fool inherits the position of keeper of love, not only because of Aphrodite's attractiveness or Hermes' guile, but also because of how folly, like love, knows no bounds. This also describes the sex of the fool. Neither male nor female, the fool is middle-sexed. On the one hand, the active androgynous nature corresponds to no earthly substance, but like the father's, mimics the quicksilver of attention. It forever calls forth our human attentiveness to mind the penchant for desire, the ground, our obligations to the earth, or Aphrodite's nature. The mix of the two yields a new gender, noted in some languages, and helps clarify our ambivalent feelings. Even when wise with love, we have difficulty in hearing the fool's voice since in it is neither maternity nor paternity.

In my research with classical origins, the fool has a curious beginning. Quite unexpectedly, the fool is related to Orpheus, poet, prophetic singer, and conqueror of hell. This may surprise you if you imagine Orpheus as wise or courageous. But his acts derive from different qualities and there is abundant evidence how he fails to follow sound advice and is reckless to excess. What impulse drives Orpheus? In him, there is an utter surrender to love. He will even descend to the underworld and bargain with its lord and lady for his lost love. We learn how he wins her, against all odds, and then, abruptly and tragically loses her. Then he must return to the earth, his home, without her whom he sought. We need to see more clearly his connection with love's fool. Looking back at a critical moment, an act that breaks the spell of her return, he is motivated by his desire for love. Love's desire that takes the lover unto Hades is a desire at heart to rescue love from its lost state. Love has died and must be resurrected—not as it was but incorruptible and no longer subject to death. This desire is the fool's also. The fool never ceases to desire love's eternity. Endless desire marks the fool's special condition. But its festering frustration goes over to a crazed wisdom, earthy, related, devout, and bizarre. The fool with stars for eyes desires most to find a passage to the stars. Yet folly is not a candidate for the astral sphere. Orpheus, unlike other ancient heroes, was never returned to the stars. Here is final proof of his liaison with the fool.

You ought not be surprised about the fool's encounter with death. Do we not make the fool's face up to resemble a death mask? What the fool Orpheus bore in him uncovers in death's own land is the core of love's secret. Without the journey, the fool remains a sorrowful clown. The desire impulse needs to be struck true to become love's desire. Nature's impulses must be remade by a higher power before passing through the dying process and being reborn as love's own. In the underworld, the fool tastes solitude. Standing alone, a nullity in the lifeless realm, the fool finds that only love stirs and speaks. In the land of the dead, there is no power greater than it. It is wrong to regard hell as loveless and we must reject the equation 'life = love,' wherever we meet it. If you recall Dante's *Inferno*, the ferryman Charon expresses surprise at the weight in his boat when they leave the near shore. It is the weight of life that the fool bears on rounded shoulders, the contradiction between magnificence and inconsequence, down to the infernal lands. In the underworld, that contradiction is undiluted. It is love's triumph to mix, the fermentation of contraries, a yeast that turns a decayed mash into the brew of living. In hell, there is desire of gargantuan proportions, but until the fool arrives, never desire for life—that is to say, love. In hell, the fool beholds loveless desires that perpetuate the dead, dream-like existence of unloved beings. Those, like the souls who experience them, are morbid phantasms. The fool see how the punishment is proportional to the desirous impulse and learns how if love is added, purification becomes possible. Love at the start, love at the end: this circle is the escape from death's death into an incorruptible mode of living.

In underworld travels, the fool witnesses many distortions of love's purification. But all pain occurs solely in relation to love. The fool recognizes that all love must suffer, but there the road divides. The left-hand path remains blind to the priceless opportunity of dying to desirous impulses and being conscious of love's ever-present origin. Here, we are condemned to repeat the cycles of Hades, never reach a conclusion, and end in blind alleyways. The road to hell is paved with unfulfilled desires. The right-hand path, by contrast, offers a living resolution. It follows a transformation of dead matter that imbues desire with fresh, revivified life. Realignment of the will with life occurs only through a voluntary death. Do you know that only a fool dies willingly? The fool's knowledge of undying love already prefigures the otherworld. This is because, guarding love's purity, the fool surrenders to death and waits for the inevitable resuscitation.

But do not be mistaken about the proceedings that I outline. The fool is no saint and goes to the end without a prayer. Fools do not pray or petition. If the eyes themselves are gifts of providence, what need is there for prayer? I do not mean to say prayer is for the feeble-minded, for the fool in many respects is that, too. But folly's perception is owned by love and dedicated to registering only what is given. That folly—by which our humanity is measured—the fool cannot delete any more than fool's words can penetrate our thick cranium. A fine apprehension of mishap's necessity, disaster, calamity, and shipwreck leave no room for prayerful exclamation. The fool respects human nature so as not to duck when the fist falls, a reflex distinct from kneeling in prostration. Here is a visible tendency toward irreverence. Strange to picture him in the foyer at the sacred temple of Eleusis, acting out ribald pantomime prior to the great initiation of the Mysteries. But for the erotic antics, initiates would not be prepared for the transformation of desire. It is curious only until you remember the fool's education in the underworld is just what the novitiates seek.

Do not glorify the fool. Folly's prescience may be the mere result of a tragic view of nature. Aeschylus, the tragedian, says, better not to be born at all, or if born to die an early death. He speaks for the fool, though the sentiment lacks an awareness of love's task, which the fool keeps. The task is beyond tragedy and comedy alike. It is otherworldly, none other than to find the elixir of life. This means, to distill love to its quintessence. The fool also is greater than tragedy and comedy put together. In the light of the great work of love, a quick end is unhelpful since longevity is a requisite to success. Yet even in a hundred years, the fool is not up to attaining it. There is no glory in the fool since the fool does nothing. The vigil is to mind the vessel while the work is being done. Do not glory the fool who is beyond glory. Folly possesses such skillful means that, lifting no finger, the incorruptible stone of love remains after death's ash is consumed.

THE STRANGER

By itself, life goes on and on. Life is continuous, without breaks, unless... Unless something enters from outside and stops it in its tracks. This is the way love arrives in a sudden vision of the beloved. Stopped, life is vulnerable, sensitized, and open to a transforming influence, where before, there was only a relentlessly forward push. Now I look across a table at the face of one I have beheld for many years. Now I am seeing for the first time and my eyes are love's. It is a rare, yet common event. I remind you of how life can be blessed by transformation.

It follows that the stranger is there, always. Only your eyes are not ready to see. What is stranger than when life is suddenly stopped? Then, you see the dream, a thin film over how things really are. With eyes of love, life asserts itself as different from thought, the way a photograph differs from a face or memory from a kiss or the rush of blood to the cheeks. Life meets the stranger and discovers . . . itself. Seeing, life falls in love with itself, and we with it. Life restored to its purity is love's object, the true beloved. The stranger brings us the true conundrum. Is the soul ever out of love?

True, the stranger appears a foreigner, hailing from somewhere far off. Foreign to the heart, the stranger holds out a set of keys to that citadel. Of unknown provenance, an alluring accent, manners that catch the eye, looks that stop the blood. The stranger is sheer attraction. It is a force, an aura that authorizes telling intimate facts about your life, secrets told only in the dark at three a.m. The stranger's command belongs to an alien presence, an outsider, one who behaves differently. Sometimes comrade of the fool, because we often see aspects of the other in a fool's appearance, the stranger stands behind the veil. We see but a strangeness that arrests us and beckons to the love in our hearts. Frail, dwarfish, bordering on the grotesque, of another species, the fool reminds us of our own difference. But the fool never brings us to a stop. The stranger, however, reminds that we are different from how we appear to ourselves—that really we are strangers to ourselves.

Who are *we*, really? That strange riddle runs through my mind. The stranger with whom we fall in love brings it with a first glance. When the breath is taken, relation becomes a force. The strange being across the café table suddenly materializes a third that exists between the two of us. We are surrounded by it. We are comprehended, and as such, come to know the other as ourselves. I do not speak of an easy or quick transformation, but of prefiguration. Discovering love all at once, we immediately intuit the end-product of this refinement I will describe. If foolishness is catalyst, then the stranger is the reagent. Though strange, love penetrates dead skin, the epidermis of habit, encrustations of security, the known and categorized, and uncovers a sensitive inside. Life lives there, waiting to experience the new touch and vibrant presence that flows through the stranger. At the core, the stranger's essence is nothing other than the influx of a finer substance that infuses an individuality. Do you recall how in myth, the stranger becomes king? The story of Oedipus is an example. It symbolizes how the stranger's arrival can transform an entire kingdom. That is the story of love, also. Love brought by the stranger shares its many gifts with our desirous nature, turning to gold everything it touches. Does this tell you who you really are?

The stranger who ignites a flame in your breast sits across in a crowded room. The room is crammed full of unseen specters, people of dream and fantasy life. Is this not how we function, with so much dead matter cluttering our souls? The stranger clears the debris with a draught of ammonia salts and we suddenly see tears through the eyes of love. These eyes behold the vivid, fresh beauty, the truth of the moment, when the pulse throbs with longing. In the gaze is the beloved. Do not be confused by what I say here. The beloved is not the stranger. Nor is the beloved you yourself. The beloved, 'hidden in the leaves, laughing excitedly,' hides the same way the whole lies hidden in each part. The beloved really involves the relation. Similarly, the whole relates to parts *as* parts and relates them *as* belonging to a single unit. In the encounter with your beloved, is not the stranger, whom you meet with love, the necessary means? The stranger is the other force, the ground, without which a current of electricity could not start to flow.

The other pole is a magnetic attraction. It is a most ancient of laws that north is drawn to south, as male to female. Together, we—I and the stranger—couple to make a whole, and apart, I and the stranger feel attraction. That force is the raw stuff of our human desirous impulse. It is powerful the way that rawness is. Call it original or primordial love, but it certainly is not love refined and glorified. That love who itinerary I inscribe for you is symbolized in the androgyne. Attraction prefigures the force that glorified love exerts on its two fissioned parts, male and female, for both feel a strong, pervasive desire for union. This is the history of conjunction, the marriage unto 'death do us part,' and the life after. Conjunction celebrates the primal dance of life, and we, woman and man, man and woman, rock back and forth. The stranger comes to carry us off to the dance floor. There, we learn the rigors of attraction and pleasures of opposition. Who is the opposite, the stranger, your partner, yourself? There, you are on the opposite side of yourself, since opposition is primarily to the self—until there is love. In truth, the self becomes a union of opposites, same and stranger, and the beloved hovers across the table. Love unites the two initially and forever after, again and again, until the dynamic stabilizes. You, the lover, and your beloved belong to two different orders until love obliterates all differences in scale and the stranger is no longer the stranger but image of love itself. This is the new Life.

Attractive force, you may know, is a cloak of the unknown. The stranger wears it, habit of a strange substance and a stranger individuality. It makes the stranger become an unexpected messenger. The message is the x in the order of things, an I-know-not-what. In all predicates of being, the stranger introduces an oblique mode. It is the mode of what-if, plot and machination and future-making. How can I be with this person forever, or at least, tomorrow? It is also the mode of disguise. The stranger is master of disguise because love must repeatedly test for the genuine, the true fool's gold. The stranger assays each truth's moment to see whether discernment is at work or merely desirous impulse. But do not think the stranger is an easy teacher. If we disregard a mistake, we may not be immediately informed since it often is wiser to let us suffer the lesson. Or, perhaps, the stranger does tell, only we cannot read the lips of strangeness and instead interpret as we wish. Either way, payment is exacted.

Of course, there are times when attraction is fatal. But they only confirm the stranger's identity as love's vassal. If trust fails, the stranger belongs on the other side of the wall. Barricades are erected to prevent entry. We play at invulnerability as our defenses are raised. We invert the energizing effect of attractive presence. Inversion, too, is lawful since there must be a force of refusal. Love is a repeated trial and requires struggle in its service. Service is not our inborn nature for we are not angels. We have a right fear of the fatality of attraction. There are demons of contradiction and warfare, dualities, and hardness. Love is not idealism and does not eradicate the devil on its way to a higher synthesis. Both sides exist, only under love, they are aligned one to the other. They have been elevated by a third. This is the holy androgyne. It is that who 'casteth out all fear' and eradicates all manner of fatality as it vows everlasting life.

I must now tell you about the process I have learned. Since any dynamic has a timing, with which we interfere by taking wrong action, there is a right time to speak directly and it has come. It is the time of the stranger. The stranger sits across the table and waits to learn how attraction leads to love. You need to give an account of a love that our two sides bear to each other and how to make it actual. The science involves a specific sequence. The coarser nature of desirous impulse must soften its stance and grow receptive to a finer impulse toward conjunction. The impulse of our finer nature, strange to the coarser, so overwhelms us as to induce a state of blackness. In this mood, life apparently turns morbid and we wish for nothing but its demise. But in the bleak night, a secret resides. Some would say, the secret of secrets. It tells that the dark womb is not barren and that an embryo grows. Soon there will be a new birth, child of love, born of the beloved in the flesh. It will give proof of how attraction of the stranger serves a divine purpose. From the union of yourself and other, a third nature, ethereal and incorruptible, comes to the light of existence.

Although strange, the stranger does not live at a distance, and so differs from the fool who does. Close like a shadow, or the shadow of a mood, strangeness follows you on the thither side of every act, just out of sight and around the corner. Until you look directly across the table, you never see the stranger—there the whole time—nor can you, any more than you can see yourself in profile. Love is like that. It takes away your breath long before you know what you are looking at. We know love by its privations and deprivations. Myth tells that tale over again. For instance, remember how the Greek moon goddess Semele tried to see her love's face—the god's—with her own eyes and was burned to a cinder by the revelation? We may catch a strange image reflected off a glass or a wet doorway—solitary, resourceful, enigmatic, powerful—but only fleetingly. Strange is that side of ourselves that lives in the obvious, ineffectual, and weak, and who unexpectedly shows up to take charge. Is it not this power you find so attractive that you fall in love with a phantom? Does love's image not pull you out of yourself, toward relation and the future birth of the beloved?

Love comes strangely from above, like the subtle luminance of the stars. If we could track it, the pathway is through a fissure in the skull, at the crown of the head. The fontanel is open at birth and never fully closes. It imbibes an ambient energy from the atmosphere, brings it to the brain and down the spinal column. Do we not speak of how love sends chills up and down the spine? We may overemphasize striving for it, which sometime works, when we find a way to be receptive. This is the will. But more often, we simply are infused with rosewater. Its shower perfumes our thought and action so that our words speak a garden. This is grace. We feel our being and its mysterious source. Love comes and changes nothing, yet everything is augmented. The strangest thing is that while the infusion brings a deep harmony, desire is truly born. True desire, an absolute restlessness, desires more of itself than can ever be given. It wants to taste deeply of its lack of satisfaction, for love can never be sufficient. Each sip only increases the wish for more and that is the nature of true desire. It opens its mouth to drink infinity in and finds it cannot open widely enough.

Impulsive desire is love on the level of the earth. It is impure to the extent it can be gratified. The impulse moves us throughout our day, when we go out, when we come in, when we lie down, when we rise up. Pure desire is perpetually on a quest to empty itself of its object and be satisfied with its lack of satisfaction. Impure desire has the inverse contradiction since to gratify it annuls its reason for being. Impure desire is friction since pursuit repeatedly rubs up against achievement and ignites a heat. This is how we move across the face of the planet. This kind of desire, though, contains an ember from the fire burning on a stranger's face. Though impelled to act through life, the fire of pure desire works its different secret on us—revealed in a flash when we fall in love and find love already waiting. The secret work of refinement smelts the gold from the dross and separates out true desire. Our rarified wish to behold the stranger who has crept in through our pores is then granted.

I do not speak of greater things. The precepts of the science say how the earth itself is elevated and redeemed in value by love. Desire has been called the hero and redeemer, the one who brings life unto life, the inner to the outer person. The wise Solomon has the great work in mind when he says, 'Hope deferred maketh the heart sick but when desire comes, it is a tree of life.' Desire's pathways crisscross the inner body and the interior of the earth. They carry life to the heart and bring well-being to the planet. Desire is love's avatar. Even the prick of lust announces the high potency of love's glorification. Even when the eye is attracted by the still-unknown stranger, love pours in to heal the loveless cares and spread its holy oil over the troubled waters. Even desire's hunger for sweets reminds us of the strangest sweet of all—to be a slave to love.

Desire is attracted to things that are attractive and drives us to and fro, seeking them. But is it forgetful of what it is for and is its search blind? Throughout, what is most desirable is to be loved. That is goodness. The good of being loved, though, is no object at all. It is a state of release into the arms of the other. What we want behind all imperfect desire cannot be attained by anything we do. *The good is our perfect undoing.* Being loved is the embrace of a pure receptivity. Desire grows more intense and active the nearer to release we grow. Like a candle melting, that is who we are. Long before being loved, you must be able. That ability is acquired in the school of desire. All I have learned says as much. You need to accede to desire without forgetting the fervor for love. Then finer matter will rain down as you hold your cup open to the fount. You will find that will be loved!

Think of the double-closed flask. As heat develops, crude matter is transformed to a thing of value. So, too, intensifying wanting something heightens desire for life and goodness. As it grows able to better distinguish life from death and evil, it turns into other than an earthly substance. It desires love, which is life itself. Alchemy teaches how the life it becomes is more vivid and less coarse than the life of impulsive desire that it was. It grows in self-reliance. It basks in being independent of powers of earth. It leads a new life that travels between the stars and the heart. The stranger is emissary to both and accompanies the new life. Thus we experience the stranger's company—this movement from our center out to the empyrean—as a second body. It is truly another organism, a desiring body and love child. Will and grace, male and female, active and receptive, all have fused. Is this not the image of love's glory? The fusion, symbolized by an androgyne, represents an attainment of the incorruptible. By this, I refer to how love's desire hungers to grow infinite and without satisfaction. Seeking no fulfillment, it can never perish. The imperishable body drinks in life that is ever-fresh and ever-young. It is the stone of the philosopher, the philosopher's son.

Love enters our body strangely, in flushes, fever, dizzy spells, light-headed feelings, and unexplained tingling. We dread its beginning and think ourselves sick when it comes. What could have vaccinated us against love? A fear of life, perhaps, and wanting things in their same old places. So we are ill-prepared and caught off-guard when the fountain brims over. Sometimes the eyes tear, or the eyes of the heart weep. The release to the desire to be loved then works its miracle. The heat from inner friction sublimates a strange substance held 'captive' like a seed by a husk. The heat, also, is of a strange sort. It belongs to a different plane, the astral, which speaks in the etymology of the word *desire*. Desire is of the starry heavens and injects earthly things with that other reality, whatever it may be. Desire's heat is that strange flame that permits the quintessence of love to condense. Even as an impure impulse, a galactic signature glows in its throb of life.

As in antiquity, the way of desire is through baptism by fire. Unlike the first baptism, by water, the fiery immersion must be officiated by yourself. In a second baptism, a second body, a body of inner desire, rises from the flames. It has properties and capabilities our natural body lacks. The fact is that unlike water, fire is of not the earth but the other world. Because it is no earthly element, metal or mineral, mercury or sulfur, its physics is different. Sun and stars are born in fire. An atom of that origin comprises an inner fire of desire. When awakened to love, a memory of its astral source stirs in us. Love comes over us and baptizes our organism with a strength to bear the intensities of the inner life.

The scale of new demands that love arouses is great. The newly baptized body must be a vessel for a transformation. One thing will meet its opposite in the combustion of glory. Do you understand how love's body needs to contain a fire that cooks all things? What the crucible holds first blackens, then blanches, as it progresses toward refinement. In sublimation, an initial attachment loosens and is replaced by a letting be. As an obsessive pursuit is sacrificed on the altar, desire to be loved—goodness itself—is revealed. The more we come to love, a higher influx penetrates the organism, with an all-pervading sensation of holiness. Desire from heart to heart reminds us time and again to open to the mysterious fountain and refresh a hidden source of inward vitality.

To look across the table and recognize the stranger as love, the eye of consciousness must not blink. What is that eye, really? You may know that it is nothing other than the heart that throbs with desire and lives for hunger and hunger alone. The heart is a hungry hunter, desiring gold 'from the stars' that gleams with the 'glint of immortality.' It is capable of finding 'such immortality as is open to a human,' as the old philosophers knew. The stranger shows how the immortal god whose vital force circulates within and warms every cell. We invite both in, stranger and god alike, and learn a hospitality suited to both mortal and immortal being. In front of both lives, dying and undying, our eyes perceive how love is a bridge and a doorway. It arcs between the two worlds, ours and the other, with the aurora of an alien light. Is this what shines on the stranger's face when, from across the table, you are shocked to find that love has called?

I will make a barter with you. The gold of desire serves as the coin. I implore you to invest a consciousness of what you really want in what you really are. Then we both may know what is truly desirable—being loved. This joy is to be found in the fountain of life. Most seek it though under differing names. You have heard how 'Energy is eternal delight,' as the poet Blake says. There is energy in loving and to love is a fine thing. To be loved is a finer and, therefore, greater vocation. Love of the heart bathes in the fount's waters, as they overflow. With the right coin, we can pay for what is free in life—if you make good the bargain. Do not stay impoverished, suffering your desires blindly, not yet being gladdened by love. I make you a barter. Will you join me in it?

Put another way, desire desires heat. What is desire but the flame of life? Even in the warm touch of skin, heat assures us love may be in the offing. Heat keeps the dead cold from us, as the dead collect, desirous of our warmth. They walk and breathe but because they have lost their vitality, they cannot feel love or especially, be loved. Therefore, the dead are without goodness and are unloved. If I sound harsh, it is because I have spent my life surrounded by their jealous souls. I may honor their memory, but they themselves are beyond my love. They cannot be objects of love because their coldness has closed them to it. That is their deadness, though miracles can happen. In a large or small way, they may return to life after a period of deadness. Let us give thanks for that, and remember *life is everywhere, the land of the dead notwithstanding.* Life passes through the land of the dead en route to the stone of the philosophers. There, it garners its incorruptible essence. The stone is what survives the region of ice, where heat of desire has fled and death itself commands the day.

Death is land of mystery and paradox. Strangely, when heat passes, desire cools and finds itself refined. How does this happen? I will explain it to you though you must have patience. Sublimation is the process of removing the fire from a substance after its time in the crucible. In its 'cold' state, desire stays youthful and ever-fresh. This is a sublime state in which desire renews its presence and fills each moment with a strangeness. It is strange how life reaches beyond toward immortal love. The essence of simplicity lies here, in the lost meaning of the alchemist's gold. Desire must die to its crude object before its real life is attained.

You must not fear love, or its emissary, the stranger. True, the stranger brings death, but be clear on this. Desire, heated to the point of being other than itself, dies. But even in death, suffering is endurable. There is no need to beseech God for mercy. The death spoke of, the stranger's death, is a conscious one. The stranger who brings love also teaches how to die consciously and be born a new thing. The map leads through purgatory, not hell. The 'dark night' is lit because desire is oriented by the pole star and the starry heaven. I do not mean that desire provides a 'tearless' path to true absolution. Salt is necessary to make gold. Sorrowing for love absent, scorned, or departed is an important theme for the students of love. Recall the Troubadours who were such students. They celebrate the lustral tears and lachrymal gold. A lover among lovers, Arnaut Daniel, one of them, wrote, 'Scarce for the suffering that I endure do I renounce fine loving, even though it keeps me in solitude.' Here is a voice that sings of the dark passage I lay before you.

Arnaut Daniel might have been familiar with school practices. In schools, they teach that to reach a state of desiring, look at each object for what it has and what it lacks. In seeing, desire's tense hold relaxes and love can permeate the sinews and bones. Through a progressive suppleness, desire is made more fluid and less snagged in accidentals. We approach the quiet inner movement of love without trying to grasp it. Desire lets love in—and love suffices when it enters. In fact, nothing else can suffice for desire and without the fragrance of love, desire is self-destructive. The gentle approach provides greater contact with the source, the fount of life, and goodness is the lawful outcome.

THE HERO

The hero of my treatise will not be apparent to your eye. Like love, the hero wears many disguises. Donning shabbiness, looking imbecilic, speaking poorly, heroism of the sort I have in mind may be fearfully underplayed. In a crowd, it disappears with no trace. In fact, vanishing is a trick of the love's hero. Just when you expect heroics, some other thing is there instead. Gradually we learn to reckon the reticence of the one who serves love without ego, for that is the hero's. In our aggressive demeanor to discover more heroism, we forget this, but the word *hero* has not. Its root affirms that heroism derives from selfless dedication to love's needs. The hero travels throughout various walks of life, attached to one thing only, service to love. Love is sought to fulfill the heart's sole desire, and that is to be a servant to love.

Why must the hero sacrifice self-will to be admitted to servitude? Do you remember how, in the story, Arthur, the king, is challenged by an evil knight who blocks the path and boasts, 'I shall defeat you.' Arthur replies, 'Whoever is to be victor is not up to you or me, but to God.' Arthur has parried his opponent's rage with unblanching truth, difficult to accept and impossible to defeat. A providence is at work in everything we undertake. It comes with its nervous companion, life, and deposits its goods on our doorstep. There is, however, a recalcitrance to rejoice in the unseen provision. A begrudging nature cuts us off from the fount and goads our self-will into subtle and not-so-subtle acts of denial. Arthur is a hero because he neutralizes the refusal with the deft thrust of his incorruptible sword Excalibur. No longer subject to a usurper's false claims, he undoes the enemy, freed to a joyful receptivity. Buoyed by love's commandment, the hero wields an unconquerable power. It does not belong to the hero and has not been gained by any deed. Girded by love and the knowledge that his doing would be its demise, Arthur grasps love's salvation. This is invincible knowledge. What can the Black Knight do but fall in the pitch of battle?

The hero's heroism is a lover's heroics. The heroic battle is to sacrifice life's impediments to love, to slew dead things in yourself, uncaring, heedless impulses. They encrust desire, which, as it tenses toward satisfaction, forgets its own imminent glorification. This is the amnesia of death. It ignores how love penetrates our earthly frame and in its wake leaves the swirl of need and want. We are impelled by desire in all that we do. Far from an ascetic abandon or saintly quieting, heroism lives in desire's full flush. The life it relishes is so replete that what follows, even if a sword's killing blade, does not distract from what matters. Heroism is perpetually of the moment, the only moment. The more deeply sacrificial it is, the more complete is its consumption of time. The hero is eternally in love with the products of time.

You may feel sacrifice as an ignition of light. When you picture the lover at work, also picture heroism as a seeker of knowledge. The preferred weapon is not an edge of steel but of consciousness that severs the illusion of identity. The lover-hero wields the lightning bolt of the enigmatic Heraclitus that can 'steer all things through all things.' Its illumination discloses false hope, cherished opinion, and self-willed value. They, the real enemy, are dispelled under the interrogation lamp. For the light source is no angelic beam from on high, but a burning question that rises from the heart and leaves the lover an insomniac. The hero asks, 'Who am I?' When an answer is spoken, it brings the sacrificial altar into view. And the next and the next. The hero is strange and extraordinary in single-mindedness. The love for the search alone disdains seduction by the sirens of irresolution. Are you willing to concede how heroism officiates at the sacrifice of finitude, the lord of boundary, definition, and limit? Its questioning knows no end and gives no repose. The hero sleeps nowhere and is at home in homelessness.

Remember how fairy tales ask, What does the lover desire? Surely, they reply, the beloved. But who is that? Here is where we need to listen to Socrates wax poetic and paradoxical. If we knew whom, would we endure perils of the way in the first place? And if we don't know, by what sign will we recognize the object of our quest? The thorny problem is solved in the way Socrates identifies the lover as the philosopher: both as one forever seeking the goblet of wisdom. The true philosopher, Plato tells, 'loves the sight of the truth.' The philosopher, moreover, differs from the wise man and sage, who already possess truth, or perhaps, is possessed by it. In the blaze of truth's glory, the philosopher's desire reveals its endlessness. The philosopher would let truth's infinite bounty fill the mortal and human ground of thought 'unto surfeit.' That is like the act of swallowing the sun. A desire to be in truth, to live in its image and be its representative, burns inside—and burns like tinder beneath the wooden refusal of a false heart. What survives the conflagration, love's fever, bears witness to heroism. The hero becomes a lover unto the stranger. Both desire nothing more than desiring itself. From then on, the hero's every action expresses a question in respect to a truth that overflows itself.

Heroism finds itself at odds with its own nature. The hero lives on the verge of departing, looking onward, beginning anew, and so continually faces a bittersweet feeling. Let us take another look at Eros. Eros, the demi-god, lives in the death of striving and dies in its attainment, only to live again when the object turns to ashes in his grasp. The hero's life is in imitation of this muscular tempo. It is as relentless and unremitting as pulsing blood. It is a ceaseless heart in quest of life's fount. Its secret nature is undeterred by failure, not because it knows all things will pass, but because the veil of service is indifferent to tragedy. Truth is the only master. But truth never shows its face to the servant. Obedient and unknowing, the servant serves one unknown and faceless. The hardship of servitude needs to be mitigated by heroic resourcefulness. To love to serve in this manner is possible only because of heroism's great need. The hero, creature of conditions, is moved to love the beloved unconditionally. Eros shares in a similar strain of heroism, Socrates goes on to tell. Did you hear of the story of his pedigree? Eros was born from the union of need and resource. On beauty's wedding day, need, scheming her way to wealth and well-being, lay with resource, then asleep in the garden. She became pregnant and in term bore love into the world. Eros takes after both mother and father and combines the most salient features of each.

To the sweet taste of desire's gratification add the bitter of an ever-receding object, and you get the recipe of heroism. Is this not the picture of Tantalus who, punished by the gods for some forgotten offense of love, stretches thirstily for delicious grapes just beyond his grasp? But the hero of love does not resemble Odysseus's heroics. Odysseus plugged his ears with wax to deafen himself to the siren call of desirousness. Desire then sang its delectable song with impunity and did not rouse irresistible longing. But Odysseus avoided the hero's celebratory toast because drinking in desire means getting drunk on love and ever-longingly for love ever finer: that love the hero would serve more fervently. True heroism waits to be hollowed out by a longing whose potency poisons the demons of hatred and loathing and purifies the body for love. Do not think that Odysseus avoided suffering and later regretted his decision. To steer the ship free of desire surrenders the most human part. Service to love does not court comfort. If we stop the ears to hardship rather than living through its transforming effects, we miss our calling. You may know how Rilke sings of love's vocation in this elegy:

> *Just as he, on the last hill that shows him all his valley*
> *for the last time will turn and stop and linger*
> *we live our lives forever taking leave.*

Here there is peace in the acknowledgement of our insomnia. If that comforts, a hero's comfort is exact in its meaning: that which fortifies the heart with love's knowledge at each step onward.

In an earlier time, you may have read Empedocles' vision of heroism. On a scale of the cosmos, he saw how love battles with discord, desire with death. He pictured two intersecting vortices and, warring, give rise to all phenomena. That is a hopeful image. It shows how love, that proper attunement of heroism's lyre, becomes active when the harmonious alignment is lost. Then a song awakens the heart. Otherwise, a listless sway of moribund feelings takes hold. With a darkening cacophony, we find ourselves in chaos, the dark before a dawn where desire evaporates in the desert of feeling. The time is again ripe for the hero. The hero is avatar of salvation. To be at the disposal of love, heroism may need to adventure to the ends of earth for the waters of life, as you know the fairy tales tell. The tasks, threefold in nature, must be met before divine rains begin and desire is restored. The trials demand anterior proof of an investiture to love. Often, black monsters have powers many multiples of the hero's, yet before the end heroism vanquishes all. This is because the hero knows the secret. What is it that makes water, softest of all things, indomitable? It is that water flows on. So when the tide of dissent reverses the lyre is retuned, as Empedocles saw. Then, love flows back to itself, flooding its holy source and revoking its opposite. The hero's intuition apprehends the play of forces. He will not set anything against the impediments but patiently abides in love's lawful return. Heroics can drink in the truth of the quest and survive the rigors of its past. The hero is the soul who does not separate from the cosmos but remains a particle of it.

Once in full stride, the quest for life's source, fountain of youth, unfolds. You will find how it truly flows with the wine of desire just as life does. Then we are flooded with desires, the desert of life flowers. This is not strange since at that time, life is no longer under attack by discord, but is being fattened with wholeness and peace. The hero's rescue saves us because then we owe nothing and are free to experience life. This once was called *participation* by the high minds of Plato's Academy, who identified hero and philosopher. They saw how desire joins—becomes a precious force in the inner life. It is the magnet that draws an embryonic being to our attention. But before desire is successfully awakened, we must rely on heroism. The hero is harbinger of awareness, and once alive, incarnate, and with a breathing body of fleshy sensations, we can tend to new life. After that, heroism no longer is needed and disappears. It returns home and grows domestic, as Odysseus was in Ithaca. Home, where love lives, waits without impatience because love knows its place in the heart. At home, the true lover, who lives in the flesh of true desire, is reborn in the movement of astral return.

A most remarkable fact emerges about the lover who stands proudly beside the hero. Or, are the two really one? Whereas the hero strives, the lover makes no effort to do the same. The lover is simply the perfect knight whose banner reads *sans effort, sans assayer*. Because of rare talent, love sees and is because it sees. Are you thinking about the two birds, 'close companions,' of the Upanishads, one of whom lives life while the other's life is simply to watch? It is strange that the lover embodies a similar duality. The two-fold heart of love sends its receptivity down to deep roots. In the midst of it, the lover opens to the mysterious influx and lo and behold, a life inside appears. This is a second life, a new nature, the embryo I referred to above, and, I tell you, is the crux of the matter. Our natural life is here to be replaced—with the hero's help—

after it goes through death. The replacement is a stranger, for its origin is not the womb. Where does it come from? Love is a self-being. It constantly refers to a glorified containment that signifies the beloved. The lover waits beside the hero—or are they the same?—arms beseeching the sky above, to return the beloved to her home in the heart. Heaven will answer the prayer of any lovers eager enough to serve.

Do you know how to wait for love? As one waits, so one also serves. 'They also serve who only stand and wait,' the blind poet sings. Love's second nature is self-creating and thoroughly independent. It seeks a heart that abides in itself, counseled in receptivity. A lover's heart knows only to serve love's labor, the great labor, and no more. But by what means? The labor may sing of desire's glorification as it returns to its incorruptible home. There, where love is keenest, the cosmos is sustained by its force. But what is love's work? Abiding, the lover welcomes the maintenance of all things, great and small. But first, the lover must awaken to the self, the new nature. To awaken, to die, to be reborn. This is the precept when lover is pupil and the self is teacher. It is most radiant in the figure of Jesus. His central tenet—'I am the way'—invokes the lover's presence and stirs a desire for the most refined of loves. He teaches how a finer current runs down the spine to animate a nature yet unborn. A remembrance on high wets our appetite for the birth. Then, the practice of transforming desire rolls back the rock before the cave of death. It becomes an observance of a new life.

In life, the lover is heroic in the face of weakness. Which lover is not weak in love? It is the hero's work to overcome weakness, and that weakness lies with judgment. Specifically, it lies coiled around the thought that you are weak and unworthy in the first place. That is actually a refusal to give praise to what providence offers. Once the refusal is incinerated, you see that you are of inestimable value. The hero works to uncover the fact. It has been overlaid by excess fascination with the world—to achieve, intend, and undertake. We are oriented toward making things happen in order to change the face of creation and prove ourselves. The impulse of desire that would metamorphose love has nothing of that flavor. It is entirely different. The lost sages remember by saying, 'desire to love is love itself.' The hero knows self-reliance. Heroism protects a wealth that invests each and every breath of ours.

If a hero does not flee a weakness, it is due to a courage to face a weakness in the self. On this point, Socrates who was brilliant at love admonishes his would-be lover Alcibiades. A great general in his own right, Alcibiades feels shame for playing to the crowd and not facing weakness. Repeatedly, he is ashamed not to look within. He had heard about Socrates' once confessing that within him were all the monsters of the earth and seas, including the greatest one, Typhon. Now Alcibiades had seen them for himself, including new ones to the underworld, the third realm. He had fallen for Socrates' courage in rejecting the lesser for the greater. Love stood barefoot in the snow during the war, and he, Alcibiades, did not escape. Socrates, however, was after other matters. He learned love from an uncompromising teacher named Diotima, which means *double temple* and refers to the forehead just above the brow. Her instructions told of the fire of desire and that it is ignited by a ray from above. With it, life burns away corruptible things, leaving the philosopher's stone behind. This is nothing other than incorruptible conscious love. It alone survives the conflagration. It was that very cataclysm that Socrates perished in as a lover and dying, found immortality. It is that very stone that Alcibiades loves in his beloved and would, if he were stronger, gain for himself.

The force of attraction provides for the philosopher, hero, and lover. They share knowledge of how heat cooks raw material and distills a higher life. From the philosopher's flask pour question after question. They repeatedly rub the thick crust of inattention the wrong way and abrade and wear it thin. That is how love works and a lover falls in love time after time simply to continue the self-inquiry, taxing as it is. We learn also from Alcibidias regarding successes and failures with his beloved, Socrates. Socrates, great lover, sought truth and the selfsame desire made him attractive to others. Being unknown, truth demands courage when faced. This the philosopher shares with the hero, who in turn understands the desire to ask after the particulars of things also. Long before Socrates, Odysseus made a meandering inquiry into the nature of things as he sought home. Time and again, he needed to verify the way and not be tricked by sorcery, holocaust, or the weather. He learned to ask after holy knowledge and know the difference in fool's gold. There are disguises, morbid and pleasant, that require foresight and resource. When he bumped against refusal, he became fortified with energy. That is what happens the lover, hero, and philosopher. All are ready to plunge onward, looking for the next question set by providence.

Movement, journey, dialectic; they go hand in hand, and the hero-lover-philosopher goes with them, a fourth. Movement refers to the fount, its basin. Receptivity, to its never-failing abundance, determines whether it affects our actions and those of people around us. Journey speaks of the pathway of better receiving, how the manifold gifts are provided. The many places in outer life correspond to inner loci. The journey quickens desire and serves to dissolve barriers to a love of life. And there is dialectic. Dialectic has a sense of *crossing over into meaning*, where its root signifies interior comprehension. Plato gives glimpses of an intelligence focussed on its prime task: to rouse desire to submit to burning away falseness. Dialectic proceeds toward the truth, and so 'true philosophers' follow it. It trains mind and heart and strengthens love. It further cultivates a power to cast morbidity of all kinds aside. The school of educating desire includes hero, lover, and philosopher, which may be one and the same. No one is born one or the other. Only on the way to a second birth can you move dialectically in love's journey.

With the hero, we emphasize the journey over the dialectic. A hero represents a 'man of action' who meets monsters with the intelligence of a swift sword. But the hero who serves love and desire lives in two places. In this regard, he might pass as kin to an alchemist like yourself whose interest lies in transmuting inner and outer. To continue the comparison, heat applied to the crucible corresponds exactly to the heat of an inner demeanor. Vision warm to the touch illuminates what the hero sees. From warmth we can draw passion. In the hero's blood there arises a white-hot flame, the heart's dedication to the call of love. You can see how this is with Odysseus, foremost among ancient heroes. As he grows more firmly focussed on home, Ithaca, love forges a resolve. Trace, from the Cyclops, through the Clashing Rocks, Circe's island, to his homeward journey, and the heat mounts. His desire for return is sublimated as his love takes a higher form. It is brought to a fine, crystalline state when it is realized in his reunion with Penelope, his beloved.

In this alchemical journey, you must be prudent and remember the task. Gold from lead, the 'coarse metal': this we know. We know also it 'takes gold to make gold.' It is a question of beginning. The philosopher remembers it takes a little self-knowledge to make a self-knowing soul. The lover knows more when it is known that attraction—desire for one's opposite—is needed for union. Attraction is the fiery fuel. It is prudent to begin to focus on attraction between opposites, male and female. Their union is achieved through conjunction, intercourse, or 'coitus.' In that act, an enigmatic exchange transpires. An intense desire achieves its object and dies. The lover lives the death through the agency of the other. This is elemental 'reciprocal fructification' and it invites a new element, mysterious and unnamable. We can speak only indirectly about it. Nonetheless, if you were to follow the process, an unforeseen result would take place. Love would give birth to its own child, other-sexed and other-worldly. Its child would vault from the house of opposition to transcend love itself.

Love lies along the restless path of desire outgrowing itself and becoming more finely desirous. It dictates how the hero must grow beyond heroism, the lover beyond loving. Besides, every hero has a measure that measures the heroism. Socrates, lover and seeker, is a fool for love in the mettle of Alcibiades. He moves beyond mere philosophy and assumes the style of the lover. Do you recall how Gilgamesh, hero of the ancient Sumerians, proclaims is love for life but humbled by sleep? He returns to his people empty-handed and no longer young, but with the verve of the philosopher. Heroism, sooner or later, turns to love. This is because the hero witnesses how deep conjunction goes and how it quickly fades into death. The hero does not confuse it with the death of endless cycles of rebirth, which is like a syllable repeated over and again. Heroism discerns how death marches through the third realm, the underworld. Neither triumph nor failure stops the hero because each death casts off another skin and reveals new life. This is not a death that shadows the heroic conquest of heaven or earth, but astral world beyond.

Turn to alchemy and there is an undetectable gap in the journey. One movement meets another at a cross-road. This is a place of the unexpected. Once at a cross-road, another hero named Oedipus meets an imperious traveler whom he kills in self-defense. A series of events is set in motion, which pushes him beyond heroics. Where one meets a second, opposite movement, a familiar landscape may give way to shades or forms of another realm. The hero walks through doors and they open to the land of the dead. If you need to image, entering a dream has a similar effect. In the underworld, events do not follow the same laws as between heaven and earth. Emerging, heroism is transformed in the very sight of life. The hero, Odysseus or Orpheus, has acquired the deathless aspect of living substance. They know a life never dies. The hero, a new being, comprehends the meeting-place of the incorruptible thing whose book is indelibly written.

From its beginning, heroism searches how to serve love. The hero's zest carries to preordained perils but allows the hero to circle back to home. But home, like that of the hero-prince of Gnostic texts, whom you may remember, is a lost memory. Love's demands have been, alas, put aside and the robes of distraction donned. Careless pleasure decorates the pattern. The prince is in danger of turning idle. Fortunately, heavenly messengers remind him. In signs, 'meaningful coincidences,' portents, and dreams, he is called from demeaning habit to the work of renewing love. The messengers are desires. They have him retrace the path, this time to new heights. For heroism, I said, sheds its skin and learns service as life, not as an added task. On his return, the prince is mindful of a commanding new identity, his own. He radiates a knowledge that returns life to its source, amplified and vitalized.

At the perfection of love's service, heroism's challenge may be more than can be met. It may require the reservoirs of the heart to open and become enflamed. As you are, heat is lacking. Even your passion is of a cold intensity. An ordinary reaction to real desire is negative and refuses it. It disturbs profoundly, you who continue in your torpor. Far from seeking it out, do you not want it stopped before it starts? For it seems to reflect a diminished state whose imperfections we allow. It may have been like this with Jesus, hero and lover and philosopher. His exquisite expression brought followers to recognize the fallen state. It also brought detractors who mistook his exalted exposition of service for a messianic or apocalyptic message. Such love was superhuman in deed since it referred to a recondite formula. It is what I here would have you study. It relates to the true elixir whose radiance lights the true philosopher's gaze. One draught and a new life is born. Its adamantine body has ties to the starry realm and it lives in service on this earth. Though his few days gave Jesus little time, we may be on the verge of recovering it. Love's perfection is attainable in this life.

LOVE'S VESSEL

From house to house, doorstep to doorstep, the lover goes. No one recognizes the stranger and the lover repeatedly meets rejection. I recall an old story for you. Once upon a time, there was an elderly couple, Baucis and Philemon, who had simple, undiscerning hearts. One day, there was a knock at the door and two gods in disguise appeared. Though fearful, they took them in and showed them their unadorned human hospitality. It warmed the strangers so that they granted the loving couple their one wish, which was for immortality. Baucis and Philemon lived to a rich old age and when they died they became two rose bushes entwined in each other's arms. But how is it in our own day when a xenophobia prevails, and the lover is guest in no person's house? We cower in fear of what the lover may expose—the heart's true nature, as it is in itself. The mute and listening heart, the heart never heard. The sting of exposure brings mortification to the ego, and that is what we strive to avoid at all costs. The lover is alien in the disclosure of human nature and its potential. The lover reminds us how human nature is that peculiar creation that has a spark of divinity within. Only through mortification does the fire flare and impulsive desires proceed toward the work of transubstantiation. Then a heart of love speaks. Its words elaborate a new substance, mysteriously distinct from coarser material. That was the second gift of the gods to Baucis and Philemen: to discriminate the act of love in all things of the earth.

The lover who seeks hospitality reminds me of an alchemist's search for a suitable vessel. A vessel is a container, something needed to hold the quicksilver of life. It must be adamantine-hard to retain an intense energy without leakage. But it must also be as soft as water and as gentle as a woman's touch or else it will harm the delicate embryonic tissue. Being a receptacle, a vessel brings thoughts of the beloved herself, and why not? It is nothing other than an incarnation of the mother-substance, namely, our fleshy body. The sensed and aware body, now prepared for loving, invites the lover in. A moment before, the body slept, in a deadened, insensitive condition. Now, the body has been awakened through an experience of desire and is moistened and maternal. Waiting from without, the lover remains alert to how the beloved is being moved by desire. The lover, in turn, grows conscious of the desire to be loved—that primary thing—and is drawn to seek entry into the vessel of the beloved. This is why the lover must knock on door after door. A desire for the being of love, for pure receptivity, is a rare thing. Is such precious desire not love itself, the very love that predates the creation by love—the love before love? Such high intimacy and complete penetration of conjunction intimates the prize the lover seeks. How can I name the name of that primordial, uncreated love? I might call it *glory*.

In its role as receptacle, a vessel functions like a cauldron or crucible. It holds the material while it heats. I have not mentioned it yet, but the fact of heat is more enigmatic than it sounds. Heat has two sources. One is a mechanical thing, a rubbing of one part against another, the affirmation against the denial. Campers can make a fire by twirling a dry stick into a board. This act is similar to trying to be receptive to something only to find that rejection or repulsion prevail. This source of heat calls intention or determination to it. There is, however, a second source, the core desire. At its core, desire is an inborn impulse and has no opposite. In itself, it is attracted and warms to the image of the lover. The more intense the image, the higher the vessel's internal temperature. Heat lies in the hollow of the heart, asleep. Fanned by the gaze on one's beloved, it begins to burn. Dante knew how the heat allowed him no choice. He had but to pursue the image of his beloved Beatrice wherever it went. He outlined the contours of his feeling as the inner thermometer mounted. Before long, he found out it is a heat that transforms matter and brings a vision of heaven. He says for us all:

> *Bearing directly on me is God's light,*
> *Piercing the bowel of my being through.*
> *Its power being then conjoined to my sight*
> *Lifts me above myself until I gaze*
> *Upon His essence whence is milked such might.*
> *Thence comes the joyfulness wherewith I blaze:*
> *My sight's intensity these sparklings show,*
> *Thus flame with vision in the balance weigh. [XXI, 83-90]*

May I say that desire warms the receptacle, our flesh and blood, and that by its action, nerves and ganglia wait, a lover in warm anticipation of the beloved? This image signifies how, for each of us, a lover's service waits. There we learn the joy of patience as we become metallic. There is also the sister of joy, sorrow, in what the lover leaves behind, lament and mourning. Both are beauties, but the voice of the Provencal poets is remarkable in combining both in their songs. Giraut de Borneil is an excellent example when he sings, 'Sweet friend, out there by the steps you begged me that I should not be sleepy but should keep watch all night until the day.' Beyond joy and sorrow is watchfulness. Giraut's fellow poets emphasis the need for a long, deep vigil. Often they compare it to a night of insomnia, when, tossing and turning, discover that an interior heat has begun to intensify. Thought is not especially lucid, though, feelings of different parts of the personality arise and pass away. It is the sensation of an organic wakefulness that stands out. This is just the first phase in an attraction wrought by desire and absence, a burning of dross. Later, I will say how the conditions for conjunction have ripened now and how the will will fall into place.

Can you doubt that nothing is more female than waiting? The act is connected in the older teaching with watching and with prayer. The 'Watch and pray,' of Jesus' sayings, refers to minding the vessel. Part of minding is to assume an inner posture that combines the hard and soft, the affirmation and negation. To find that middle requires a vigil and a gaze wide, pliant, and yielding. The only thing we know about love is that we know nothing. Its movement is unexpected and surprises us. We see how constancy is in demand in the face of a deferring of impulses. This is the waiting I mean. In waiting, we attend to the very display of attention, which is devotion. This refreshes our vision for it works the way love does since it *is* love in the way it works. This is positive aspect of waiting, which is what the vessel does. This makes patience most sought and most needed when dealing with containment or constraint. Patience holds distractions back so we can look outside in search of a vivifying vision. That is what another favorite of the Troubadours of mine, Guildhem de Montanhagol, discovers when he looks across the table: 'He who sees your fresh complexion, fair one whom I adore, and your bright eyes and their delicate lashes of natural splendor; every man loses ill-feeling if he beholds you, beloved.'

There are, for the sake of completeness, negative aspects to waiting. They have to do with keeping the vessel pure. This is not easy. There are many monsters that eat at metal, so-called 'impurities' that infect the eye and ruin the ear. They want the material of your little stove inside, where you are conducting your experiment. They are basically mindless and can be dismissed since they mean no harm. But you need to be firm in your act or the monsters may do outrageous things to catch you. Then, suddenly, your waiting is over and your patience spent. You find yourself in need of a clean vessel.

As we are, we are mostly unable to wait. Certainly, we are far too impatient to watch over the inner fire. This fact tells us that the female is lacking in development. Because of this, the vigil remains incomplete and the prayer unuttered. With the eye closed and the tongue wooden, what can the state of desire be? Can it ever be cultivated since force will do it no good? This is a paradox of movement, but not an impasse. Or, if it is an impasse, it is one with an experience of remorse. Remorse comes after a time that pretension ruled love. At that time, arrogance also maintained that it knew how. It cannot happen often enough that our usual state of affairs, governed by the paradox, is suddenly cast aside by the tide of events. Then, an unrequited attraction, a bitter rejection, scorn of the other, ridicule at exposure, an unexpected incompatibility, these comprise the slap of wakefulness. Arrogance pays for its presumption and we accept how our limitations show. The eyes 'wet with weeping,' go joyful at this kind of payment. In the tears is then found a rare salt. It is the same salt that through repeated soaking turns the bitter skin of the orange to sweetness. Remorse resembles that salt. It seasons a crust over ourselves and gradually dissolves it. Beneath you find a tender skin, sensitive from being a part of our truly human condition. Remorse lets us attend before patience comes, along a slow maturation toward love. In this ripening phase, the sacred desire, the desire for being loved, can grow apace as it was unable in earlier development stages.

Tempered by waiting, our vessel grows trustworthy. The vitality-sapping schemes of the ego that corrode the metal diminish as soon as trust appears. In this regard, nothing is more to be trusted than a cleansing by remorse. The chief feature of remorse is a cleansing of vain machinations. This allows for a certain house-cleaning to take place. We are less anxious to take on airs. Then, as we practice receptivity, the female essence strengthens. We are durable enough to bear the sight of how empty life is without desire. Then the paradox appears and desire becomes precisely what we lack because we believe we have it. In the paradoxical light, we grow more patient yet. We cease to delude ourselves into thinking we can give anything. When we dare to, we find nothing is there because our vessel is leaky. It holds nothing. If we do not recoil in shock, we witness Empedocles' great discovery in action. As soon as we get it fixed, what is hollow fills with desire from its holy origin. Before long, in the vessel, a warming wrought by remorse takes place. There, new life reticently stirs.

A lover goes in search of hospitality and seeks a home. It must be a structure sound enough to contain a desire to be loved. Day after day, the lover knocks on the door, begging to be let in. Strangely, one day the door opens and then, the lover discovers, from the inside. In this state, preliminary to the act of love, there is a foretaste, a prophecy. At last the lover is serious about the quest, the philosopher likewise with the question. From beginning to end, the lover meets only the presence of love. Before the journey, the lover was chided for failings and played expectations down. The lover is like Narcissus but also not like him. Remember how wherever Narcissus peers into the pool's mirror, his image was returned to him. He was lost to it and mistook the beloved for someone other than himself. The lover is not like Narcissus in how, when inside the vessel, things take a different perspective. The lover, now purged of self-concern of any kind, is ready to meet another. This point is precisely where the stranger comes in. The stranger carries an unknown book. It is the book of attraction

Who is the stranger and what does the book contain? An answer arrived at only after the vessel is free of leaks and cooks a while. There are ways to describe the process, but mine is a story. It begins with one day there is a knock on the door. From inside, a voice asks, 'Who is it?' 'It is I,' the reply comes. 'Then begone!' With real despair, the one who knocked went away. That one found the road of return long and arduous. Eventually, however, he comes to the door and knocks again.

'Who is it?' comes the voice inside. This time, the book replies, 'It is you, my beloved.' 'Since you art I, come in. This house does not have room enough for two.'

I am back to the matter of hospitality. Hospitality is an act of honor. You honor the wedding bed, where desire meets its opposite, the object. Here, conjunction is meant to take place. The owner spent time cleaning rooms, opening windows, and setting out flowers of devotion. Time passes and no one comes. The lover comes to see she is not yet eligible for marriage. Unsure of herself, she calls around and sets out emblems of her calling. But you can see she as yet does not know what is up to her. Furthermore, she has not been called by the right voice, or if she has, has not heard the sound. She endures deprivation and suffers. This state is the hidden heart of hospitality. It is when no guest comes. Instead, the state of mortification comes. In it, indescribable changes take place in her. There is a softening of metal and becoming more womb-like. I must tell you about these changes later. In the story, she ages and becomes quiet. One day as she is occupied with the daily round, there is a knock at the door. The door opens and . . . .

Who is the guest, the beloved, for whom the vessel is in wait? He leaves only a trace to suggest the identity of an enigma. His sound is a whisper in the dark that calls us to rise up and wake. While he is beside, joy abounds. There is hope and we revere the way things are. Naturally, we grow curious to see his face in the clear morning light. He does not permit that. He is gone before our eyes, a breath of wind trailing out the door. The day fills with longing for his presence and evening contains sadness at his absence. Why will he not let himself be seen? This question prompts many to reflection. Apuleuis in the second century is a favorite of mine when it stirs his imagination to fashion the story of Psyche and Eros. The whole thing is about whether it is an intrigue of the beloved, an adventure in desire, or mere whimsy? When Psyche, the lover, steals a look at her beloved, he is gone, an enigma. Was her vessel faulty? What must be done? To regain him, she undergoes trials. It is the last I find most interesting. In it, she is a traveler to the land of the dead. She goes to ask a favor of its queen. In this way, she indirectly gains the gift of immortality together with her beloved Eros. The vessel had to be broken utterly and remain anew.

In an ancient dance, the beloved descends with the lover's ascent. The movement, its expression, and its consummation are all necessary for conjunction. The beloved comes down by grace, an advent beyond effort and intention. The heavenly fount opens and pours its vivifying waters in true abundance. But unless the lover reciprocates, her nature uplifted by the invitation, no movement ensues. Neither is there expression nor consummation. The earth stays parched and barren, a wasteland. Percival, fool and lover by title, is tongue-tied and omits asking the one question of the Fisher King. 'How art thou?' By whose will and under what power are you if you are who you are? Without being invited to respond, the King remains paralyzed. He cannot bestow his beneficence and Percival, the lover, is banished from the kingdom. Castle and royal domain disappear, lock, stock, and barrel. As grain fields languish and wounds fester, Percival takes on the role of a wanderer and spends his lifetime looking for the castle door. At last, he is back at the Fisher King's and addresses him with his question. By that act of fecundation, nature is allowed to ascend. The twin currents bind heaven and earth in mutual fertility, like lover and beloved. Conjunction is symbolized by this exchange. For through it, the mysterious conditions for the birth of incorruptible substance, the grail, once again exist. The stone is born through the vessel.

Do you wonder whose birth this is? I think it is the one who is present whenever two of us meet in his name. What do we call him? Saint Esprit, perhaps, or the Holy Ghost, an other who bears witness to the lover's joining the beloved. According to ancient law, a third element is needed to complete the picture at desire's perfection. Real desire is perfected when its unattainable object — being loved — is attained. At the moment that desire breaks the bounds of possibility and turns into love, a new, incorruptible consciousness erupts. Others say that the ripened fruit of desire is none other than the wisdom sought by philosophers. Wisdom goes beyond mere words for it can be handled, felt, and used wisely. In the spirit of prophecy, Solomon says: 'Wisdom is a strength to the wise man more than ten rulers which are in a city.' In wisdom, contradictories are reconciled and worked to support the other. Fine and coarse, high and low, male and female: oppositions brought together under the auspices of wisdom relate to one another. Through wisdom, war is ended and peace prevails. Lover attracts beloved through this mysterious work. Attraction is an intermediate means. Once consummation occurs, it is transcended in a deeper unity. The inner life born—wisdom incarnate—reveals a paradoxical aspect. Wisdom, fruit of desire, must have been on hand at the very start, though in no way apparent. Regardless of the strength of attraction, lover and beloved could not reach across to each other and conjoin were it not for a strange wisdom. There are images of lovers who forever gaze longingly at each other across an unbridgeable chasm. For them, they never moved beyond attraction. Wisdom, being uncreated, is like a toast that commemorates the sacred marriage. It is the 'blush that marks youthful vigor' and makes pleasure both pleasurable and wise. I would say wisdom is father and mother of the birth that is wisdom, too.

If you look back in time, ancient law tells that wisdom has no opposite. There is wisdom in all things and no thing is without it. Wisdom is, therefore, unique in this world for even the beloved meets resistance when he comes to call. At times, the lover leaves the door locked and the house closed to strangers. Fearful, anxious, overly concerned, involved in pettiness, or consumed with vanity, the lover forgets to tend the tree of life. Then she isolates herself and in confusion takes the lesser for the greater and the worse for the better. We inhabit the realm of relativity where each thing has its shadow, it's not-self. Pure affirmation—what the beloved seeks—is scattered in streaks in an impure ore. It remains a trace element, a possibility. The lover is a mixture. She lives with denial as well and longs for the end to her infernal conflict. Wisdom has a different constitution. Unlike affirmation that calls negation forth, or negation that addresses the positive, wisdom is a balance. At equilibrium, it alone stands alone. It is always and everywhere yet because desire is still unrefined, we see nothing but the object. This is the condition of the philosopher who sets out to find the third thing that penetrates the heart at every point. Wisdom enters intangibly and without words, a caress at the nape of the neck. Turning to look, you discover your pleasure, desire's fruit, is invisible, a secret influence.

As it stands wise and alone, wisdom is not opposed to folly. The true fool does not regard folly apart from wisdom but lets it in the back door instead. The fool is wary of lover's wiles. It is a fool who forgets how tenderly love is received while desire is young and robust. As soon as desire ages and slackens, the real battle for patience begins. The war pits the soft against the hard, the quick against the slow, the mighty against the meek. The fool is aware that patience is the cloth of wisdom and alone brings peace between warring parties. Wit, humor, and irony are helps. This awareness isolates the fool from the rest of humanity. Folly, like wisdom, stands alone, as I said, in the daily round as the world spins. Knowing the play by heart, the fool stands outside it, not lover, not beloved, exercised by each, pitied. Perhaps because the influence remains indirect, the fool does pratfalls for the wise. We must look for a hidden meaning, therefore, when Solomon speaks ill of fools:

> The words of the wise spoken in quiet
> Are heard more than the cry of him that rules among fools.

In truth, the two stand on common ground that is holy. When fools speaks of love, their words light on traps the lover has set for herself. Revealed, the doors burst open and the beloved can enter. Wisdom finds a way in along with the prattling of foolishness. That is the way all manner of things can be set right with the world.

Into the lover's house, tended now by patience, her beloved comes. He is not one but has many faces. Along with wisdom, desire to be loved is admitted. In the act of conjunction, love and wisdom come to dwell in one house. What house is this? The lover's house is her body, that temple of the god. It is also a template of the starry region. Veins and arteries and nerve ganglia are maps of star fields—or, alternatively, antennae by which transmissions from those distant beings arrive. Strangely, the higher frequencies seek to be heard by our organism. It is providential that the body is desired by those wiser beings in whose image it was made. You must bear this fact in mind for it is the reciprocal of the lover's desire to be loved. You are here at work because your work is needed on high.

David Appelbaum

I am my beloved's
And his desire is toward me

sings the Shulamite woman of *The Song of Songs*. It is her body that she prepares. There are perfumes, oils, and powders for the outward senses. Applying them, her body becomes more attractive. But this is only the visible part of her preparation. The unseen part makes her body hospitable to the force of the beloved. She, too, engages in a work on desire that I commend to you. So she sings:

I was asleep, but my heart waked:
It is the voice of my beloved that knocks, saying
'Open to me, my sister, my love, my dove, my undefiled.'

Ancient laws of hospitality require us to help the guest feel at home. We must invite the guest to take our place by the hearth. The awakened body performs the act without hesitation since its knowledge comes from an unlearned source. You must know by now that the awakened body is the vessel proper. Our cells are the very matrices of its metal.

Into the rarefied, sensitized body of the Shulamite, the beloved waters of life pour. Baptism occurs, setting the stage for conjunction. Desire is about to bear fruit and imponderable wisdom be reborn. But the philosopher's stone is not so easily obtained! The catalyst is missing. The gift for the gods, mark of blood on the door post, ash on the brow: there is a payment to be made. The eyes need to be wet with weeping. The bitter salt of remorse is required as long as the heart locked shut. That is when the lover's body remains unwarmed by the call. The Shulamite laments,

I opened to my beloved;
But my beloved had withdrawn himself and was gone.
My soul had failed me when he spoke.

The first work I tell you of is to render the body fit for love. As it is, it is preoccupied with conquests in the world. The new posture must be like a reed, pliant and compliant—warm with desire, like petals, the pores open. Consciousness blends with sensation in the foreplay of conjunction. But then, there may be a backward step. Resistance may stir, hardness may return along with a defensive crouch. The gesture of hospitality needs practice over and again. Like the love it invites, it is never completed. It is never complete because, as the lover discovers in consummation, it is already complete. But since she partakes of both realms, earthly and astral, relative and absolute, her body mixes coarseness with purity. Is not her wavering the basic rhythm of human love, the undulation of the hips and spine, the tremor of the lips and tongue? Do we not sway with desire? Do our knees not tremble? We 'fly between the two worlds,' as spirits or emissaries of love while the vessel's metal is tempered with strength.

The lover's remorse as well as joy stems from a dual nature. Her habitat, with its dark and light, rich and impoverished, airy and close, is also where the beloved, without qualities, would come. There are hidden harmonies but they must be released. The attunement is up to her only in part. Clarity about limitations comes after the eyes have been cleansed by tears. The impurities need to be leeched from impulses of desire. The special heat of remorse—like the action of salt on healthy skin—removes the astringent taste of self-will. It is this that drags hope down and dampens fluid motion. As bitterness abates, the lover is better able to take flight, to accept absence or celebrate return. Her contentment with what she really has is her joy.

THE LAND OF THE DEAD

I have told you how the impulse of desire lives in its own death. Born with a restless nature, desire flourishes by seeking what is beyond it. At its essence is a strange hunger. It would be satisfied with dissatisfaction. Its image is the open palm. At odds with itself, it remains happy as long as it does without. As soon as it wins its object, it languishes and dies. It lives for nothing else. Each time, it rises from the ashes of its discontent and sets off to find what it lacks. Do you see the image of the phoenix latent in desire? I will tell how to materialize it.

There is a monotony to the endless repetition, but each time, desirous impulse says the same. 'Let me be loved, let me be loved,' it cries out. Once desire is garnered with love, it lives forever. The cycle of birth and death is over, once and for all. We saw how barren it remains in that condition. In order to germinate and bear fruit, it, like a seed, must undergo death. Unlike the lilies of the field, the death I speak of does not belong to the natural order. Only a conscious death allows desire to perfect itself. The fruit of the impulse, I said, is a rare growth. For this to happen, desire must awaken to its hidden dynamic and its glorious potential—and die. Impulsive desire is obsessive and blinds us to its senseless repetition. We must see our way out of wanting the same thing over and over again.

To awaken, to die, to be reborn, fertile and fecundated, is the ancient teaching on the heart. You know how the arousal of attraction leads to conjunction, after which male and female enter the death state. Here they invoke the play of underworld mystery. It is recorded since earliest history how a new consciousness is induced through its practices. The nucleus of them concerns love in a pure form. Love is their holy of holies. The drama portrays impulsive desire as drinking from the fountain of life while the couple sleeps the sleep of the dead. There is more to the picture than meets the eye.

What I will tell you about conscious death has been symbolized since antiquity. It is represented as a journey to the underworld, the fourth realm that lies beneath the other three, the starry sphere, heaven, and earth. It is referred to as the land of the dead, but is also thought to be the realm of dreams and of thoughts yet to be born. To cross while alive and conscious is possible, but full of peril. You can look at Dante's example. In the *Inferno*, when he steps into the boat, he is admonished by the ferryman Charon, who carries dead souls to the other shore: 'And you who are living yet, I say begone from these who are dead.' Only the intercession of Virgil, his guide, saves Dante from being refused passage across. There are other examples of danger. For instance, Odysseus is forewarned and descends only with special provisions needed to fend off the monster who guards the gate. And there is Psyche, of the story of *Psyche and Eros*, who also is instructed in a secret entry by which to safely find the underworld. All three examples tell how special knowledge is required. Otherwise, death means mere indifference and a lifeless, wooden condition. The warning that Dante places over the entrance to hell, 'Abandon all hope ye who enter here,' speaks to those in an unmindful condition. Let us be mindful of the dark region we are about to penetrate.

The night journey presents another grave danger. Even after all obstacles, the greatest is becoming other than oneself. That would seem to involve loss of the selfsame prize one seeks. What should such a calamity occur? Love alone suffices to explain. For the seed of desire to pass through an interval of death and bear fruit, love must bear it forward. It is a matter of right attitude. A love of consciousness remains wakeful while desire is put to death. It is like the falcon that warms the nape of the pharaoh's neck. It keeps watch over the embryo in the seed's core as certain unusual influences stream in. It bears witness as life transforms into that which is yet to learn of itself in the heart of darkness. It is a conscious love that I speak of. It has the understanding of the underworld process called mortification.

During mortification, the living person must bring to light all that is dead within. This happens when the soul is placed under such intense interrogation that one cannot hide. With mortification, there arises the feeling that there is no place to hide. We then see how we only pretend to be alive and avoid feeling that we are not. Feeling I do not really live is the heart of mortification. The realization that our so-called life really belongs to the dead and not the living has the effect of deepening love's search. For we discover a need for life and that there, we ourselves are needed to breathe life into deadness. Pretension withers as we expose layers of ourselves. There is less to worry about as we walk through the underworld. There is the primal fear—connected with our survival—of acknowledging a deeply concealed aversion to life. Before mortification is over, we need to understand the fear. On the lookout for knowledge such as this, heroes of yore braved black caverns in the land of the dead and emerged totally transformed.

At its darkest, life is so averse that mortification can find no purchase. There, no amount of self-will can end the hiding or arouse a taste for truth. In this region, we rely on assumption and stay without question. Life remains frozen in rigid patterns. Dante depicts the strict terms in hell as the inhabitants repeat their desires as punishments. The lack of variation to their action is the form retribution takes. Their attempts at satisfaction are empty yet their striving is repetitious. Still, they fail to grasp the contradiction of unattainable satisfaction and that ignorance deepens their bondage. Mortification is no possibility to those who are mindlessly punished, though they may suffer unenduringly that way. Instead, mortification is a more advanced standing and requires conscious suffering. Suffering is conscious when we come out of hiding, at whatever cost. If you look at Dante's thought, this represents a step beyond senseless pain. He alludes to conditions of purgatory that are more favorable to transformation. Purgatory is an underworld realm where beings recognize their morbidity and work to transform it. Do not be attached to the literal meaning of the underworld. Purgatory is a part of the interior world. There is a lower purgatory where the psyche's feelings are refined. Here an alignment with the nature of the being is restored. The upper purgatory involves remorse about which I will say more.

Although many speak of the first purgatory, only one myth refers to the purgatory of remorse. This is why I tell you the story of Orpheus. Orpheus, alone, speaks about the second purgatory, its upper reaches, and what emerges from the far end of the journey through it. In Orpheus's plight, this purgatory is said to foster a special vision. The vision is a vision of deprivation. Orpheus embodies it when he shows how one is deprived of the beloved. Furthermore, the vision explains how only oneself is responsible for such an act. No one stands in between you and your beloved. Orpheus is an image of self-deprivation. Do you see this? In the account, Orpheus struggles against heavy odds to accomplish his mission in the land of the dead. It was there that he must bargain for his beloved Euridyce and the right to bring her back to life. Their love consumed both until she was bitten by a venomous snake. His only weapon is his song and with it he is sublimely successful. All parties agree to her return if he can look away from her until they are safely back. Can he expunge the underworld abode from his mind? He leads her upward until an absent glance toward the gate of purgatory overtakes him—he forgets his vow. Behind him, Eurydice disappears forever. When he comes to his senses a moment later, Orpheus has only himself to blame. He then becomes a vessel of remorse. Salt flows in great plenty. When he finally emerges from this second purgatory, Orpheus is for us the primordial hero of remorse.

When you come to the land of the dead proper, you are in second purgatory. Only there does mortification have a purpose. Otherwise, it is akin to self-flagellation. The idea is to expose essence. Ascetics spoke once of a 'mortification of the flesh.' Before a literal-minded bias took hold, *the flesh* referred to the bundle of assumptions one held. It was what got *fleshed out* in the course of living. The assumptions define a world known to me and a world that defines me. These are one and the same world. When assumptions are exposed—through mortification—a new sense of choice emerges. It is not so much choice over a course of action as it is choice of self. It involves being decisive about who I am. This is the I that shines through the rent fabric of assumption that is the habit of life. In mortification, the dress of the ego is not so terribly important. Its tyranny is deposed. Orpheus, the hero, who suffering the encounter with his own nakedness, expresses the way for us.

In the story of Orpheus, there is a strong element of fate. Fate says, 'It could not be otherwise.' It was so to speak ordained from the beginning that he would regain his beloved and lose her through inadvertence. This explains why Orpheus is a hero of remorse, because remorse has to do with inevitability. It is a response to an inevitable and will-less withdrawal from love. Remorse takes you to an experience of the underworld where you meet the demand for payment. In the glaring light of consciousness, you suffer a lack of awareness of what matters.

This is a special retribution that changes nothing in the outer situation but has a strong inward effect on the sufferer. Here, you need to consult books on the great work, but I will give a clue. It gives you the means, in Dante's words, for 'human spirits to purge themselves, and train to leap up into joy celestial.'

When we look at the story, Orpheus is consumed by remorse and does not fully emerge from it. Perhaps it is this that makes a hero of remorse; he defines the experience of the dead. Because he never surpasses death, he shows homeopathically how the dead must bury the dead to make way for the living. Bitterness is drawn from the heart, which made it sick by deferral. There is the hoped for result, as Dante describes it, that

> Brought to my eyes renewal of delight
> So soon as I came forth from that dead air
> Which had oppressed my bosom and my sight. [I, 14-18]

For Orpheus, it is otherwise. The walk through the dead land is endless in that it follows him to the end. Hero of remorse, he is unable to quit mortification for the life it promises. He remains inhospitable and unreceptive to the prospect of being loved. It is fitting how, in the end, we see him torn to shred by Maenads, wild furies of feminine nature. Did he not refuse to don the female nature and let the beloved come home? Is that not his mortal sin?

Ordinary desire, impulsive desire, is alive only as long as it stretches toward its object. It then succumbs before proceeding to another object, and another, and so on. The underworld journey demonstrates the moribund nature of desire. Desire is nothing more than a compulsive craving for something different. It does not doff its disguise and we never behold its essential energy that is 'eternal delight.' Because of its misalignment, it robs us of vitality. Real desire is a whole other creature. It thirsts for what flows from the fountain of life. It seeks to drink the finer rain that descends from the stars. Toward that golden elixir is where I am directing you.

Mortification belongs to the alchemist's laboratory because it transforms 'base' desire into its heavenly counterpart. But it does not happen without effort. One who follows the hero of remorse needs to practice loving 'the sight of the truth'—come what may. This is the means to set the salt of remorse ever more deeply. Otherwise, its saline action only comes into contact with surface phenomena. But do not let your heart feel turmoil. All that is done in love's name is not ceaseless activity. Passion for achieving the stone needs to be balanced by a passion for quiet. Only in the stillness does the pearl of conscious suffering grow. It is there, humble and glorious, ready to show itself to all creation, when remorse has finished its work   That is the moment the shell opens and the treasure is revealed.

Once desire is awakened, it is able to die and be reborn in an incorruptible form. The journey through the underworld must, therefore, be attended by love from the start. That is the paradox I present to you: love is the alpha and the omega. If it is not an ingredient, the soul suffers without issue or reward. Love is the enigma. Love is in search of love. It has been kidnapped to the realm of the dead. Isn't it the eternal mystery story I am reciting? It has always told and always will of a love diminished and made sorrowful by a loss of itself. In archaic form, Isis brings her beloved Osiris back to life by collecting the pieces of his mutilated body. In another form, closer to us, Demeter rescues her abducted daughter Persephone from the jaws of Hades. Love expresses the relation between mother and daughter and the desire each has for the other. One day, Persephone is torn from Demeter, abducted, and wedded to the king of the dead. Demeter, whose love brings fructification to the earth, must descend and negotiate her safe return. While she is there, field and meadow turn into a wasteland. No fruit or grain ripens. Her departure from life means death to the earth. All living forms are cut off from the precious emanations from the stars. The desire of no creation can be transformed into love.

In the story, all life holds its breath in anticipation of what will happen next. Demeter lives in the land of the dead as one of the dead. She hires herself out in the king's court as a governess. She partakes of a deadness the living never know and becomes like a figment in a dream. She is without living desires. Cut off from the fountain of life, she is not dead, but a life negated by some perverse act of will. For us, Demeter in her predicament represents love divided and turned subterranean. This occurs when love is prey to a dark attraction of the underworld and held captive there. Then, although love is the key to evolution, on its own it is unable to free itself. The three higher realms suffer from stagnation. Strangely, there is neither birth nor death, germination, growth, or harvest. Only the stars in the empyrean, whose courses are fixed, continue in motion.

But their light does not reach the lower spheres of creation.

In great lamentation from the earth, the gods and goddesses are called to council. They are concerned because their temples are empty, their worship forgotten. By edict, a compromise is reached. The law of proportion must be obeyed. To the degree that Persephone has eaten the food of the dead, she must remain in the underworld. To the degree she has abstained, she is free to rejoin her mother. As it turns out, she has swallowed only a few pomegranate seeds, so for the majority of the year, love is whole and fructifying. But love has its winter, also, when it is cold and without interest in living. At that time, it is like unto dead—in a state of mortification. Then is the reign of the white goddess. Winter is, however, only an interval prior to spring. The death-like suspension of life is a preamble an on-going fulfillment of love. The story tells how love must pass through its black period in order to regenerate itself on a higher plane. For, after Persephone's return, Demeter knows of their inevitable separation. Her knowledge of finitude intensifies the desire to relate to her daughter and carries her love to a new height.

The mystery school of Eleusis kept the curriculum of Demeter's journey intact for ancient Greece for a thousand years. Any person who spoke Greek could participate and undergo the experience of initiation. Although the precise nature of the schooling was a closely guarded secret, we can surmise that the drama of love's forced separation was somehow enacted in each participant. Through ritual means, each one along with other participants, quit the earth and descended to the land of the dead. There, like a hero or heroine of yore, each had commerce with the dead, was touched by their condition, and felt death. Each one searched for love's missing heart, which corresponded to what blocked the full flowering of one's essence. At a climactic moment, love's wholeness—mother reunited with daughter, daughter with mother—was rediscovered. For participants, it was a cathartic moment. All at once, the gate to purgatory had been breached and the mount of purgatory ascended. Small wonder the sparse written record of the experience points to how individual lives were marked by transformation. Eleusis was a field where the beneficent action of death was yoked by courageous heroes for the sake of growth of being.

LOVE'S WORK

Do you still question the fact that love has work to do? Do you think it is just a spontaneous play, an exchange between opposing pairs of forces? Love may be that, but we humans grow up with inhibitions. While play may be kid's stuff, it takes us a long time to grow young. In shedding olds skins, we start with the outermost one, which is the thickest, and work in toward the more sensitive. Our real skin is underneath the crust and pulses with health and vitality—with life. It is the skin of our essence. Think of it as the tissue that encases the heart, the endocardium. I am speaking of a heart that has been wounded. It is a heart that must remember its need for healing and must, therefore, have heart. The work I speak of, the work of love, is to remember the heart.

The objective of this special work can be simply put. In fact, simplicity is the only way to say it. You need to work in order to love life as it is. The work is to cultivate a desire to live, not on your own terms but on life's. The attitude you need to adopt calls for an emptying of impulsive desires. They radiate from the self-will and desire to take charge and be in the driver's seat. They get in the way of taking things in accordance with life. Because of an inherent blindness, they make you insensitive to the tempo and rhythm of events and leave you out of phase with the flow. Because of their self-absorption, they block the impression of how thirsty you are to drink from the fountain of life that pours its bounty upon us. They cause an amnesia of the one source of things both masculine and feminine, light and dark, empty and full. You find yourself frail and starving, a soul without provisions.

The work of love centers on the heart because it alone can nourish self-desire in its emaciated state. The heart responds to a loveless, under nurtured existence life, the way a mother does her sick child. Its response knows the one thing needed. The one needful thing is a receptivity to the source that provides everything. The heart needs to take in the source's provisions if it is to become healthy. This means, simply, that the heart must let itself be. Strange to forget, when the heart can only be itself. Yet, to let this be done, it must rigorously balance two quite different disciplines. It must relinquish fear and it must hold to trust. One looks to the past while the other, to the future. In this regard, self-desire expresses a negative reaction to fear: one builds defenses and fights wars. If there is no negative reaction, fear may be there but withers away, a neglected waif. Trusting the events unfolding grows to be the more important thing. Trust shifts a focus stuck in the past to one of the present moment. It allows us to feel at the center of things, which is in the heart. The heart means the center. What comes from the center is always love, and what revolves around the center moves in the orbit of love.

Now you are ready to consider mortification. Its net effect is cleansing. The heart's tissue has been cleansed of diseased cells and is then ready for implanting healthy ones. That love's work can take place only after the cleansing means that it begins further along than we usually think. Cleansing the tissue brings more energy, which is needed for the phenomena of love to show itself. In the light of a cleansing, each loved thing stands forth as what it is. It no longer has its outlines confused with other things, in the confusion of indifference, ambivalence, or hatred. This is especially important since the confusion is oneself. After walking the land of the dead, as Demeter did, one is in a position to observe the turbidity of confusion and see what is taking place. The net effect of mortification is optical. It clears the eye hidden underneath the morbid tissue of a sick heart.

When the scales fall and the eye clears, you see into the heart as well as from it. This is strange because the heart is transparent. Seeing into it is like seeing the limpid atmosphere whose transparency separates the eye from the object. You see what ordinarily is invisible. You then understand how the heart is really a medium, a vessel to contain an experience of a very high order. When sight is cleared of distraction, it comes from the eye of the heart. You then know that the meaning of life has to do with looking toward an ordinarily unseen source. That look, as it illuminates each phenomenon, vitalizes your essence. Once in ancient times, it was known that mortification has to do with drinking from this dry spring. Now we need to remind ourselves how this is true: by seeing with the heart's lucid vision, we become precisely what we are and are meant to be—physicians of our own love of the source of life.

Cleansing the heart, we let the soul swell to its normal size. No longer weighed down by a morbid presentiment that deadens its self-impression, it can drink deeply. Impulsive, self-seeking desires do not contort its lips. Its mouth is free to open to the overflowing source that shatters all death forms. Although the soul's liberation is an important event, it is not the heart of the matter. That concerns the spirit. The flux of vital material from the font fills the thirst of spirit and the spirit thirsts for more. A stream of life-energy flows down from above, irrigating its folds. The spirit's desire is other than an impulsive one and can never be satisfied. Even when it is refreshed by the stream, the spirit desires more even more desirously. Here is where we find the fruit of love's work, the labor of cleansing the center. It has to do nothing but desire. Desire withholds any motion that interferes with receiving the contents of the stream, and further whetting the desire for more. Yet this is not selfishness because in the simple receptivity is a perfect expression of gratitude.

What a strange work love is at the beginning. When does it start? Although there is much to be endured in the underworld and before, the end of remorse marks the real onset of labor. Look at some classic examples. Take Odysseus who undergoes many hardships before descending to the land of the dead. Once there, he must make a strenuous effort to keep the dead souls at arm's length, for they hunger for living blood. All this is a penance. The work for love—returning home to his beloved Penelope—is possible only after his return to the earth. Then, having absolved himself of debts owed his dead mother, his soul can swell to its proper proportion. His spirit is then sufficiently unencumbered to receptively dispose itself. This is when work can begin in earnest. The lover, feminine in its nature, can unfetteredly express desire for the beloved. Waters from the font pour in, further fructifying his resolve, rounding out his heroic humanity, and speeding him on his way. But notice how the effortless labor runs contrary to almost every human impulse. Odysseus, symbolic man of action, must subdue the desire to take charge and instead let the providential will rule. In the act of submission, he uncovers the real work of love. He is a transformed being by the time he arrives home.

The impulse to take charge motivates all self-seeking desire. You can recognize it as a desire to conduct yourself as though you were a source of action. Taken by impulse, we grow insensitive to the energy overflowing from above, which acts on and through us. Even the cells of our bodies are affected by its penetration. But we are poor hosts, forgetful of the obligation of hospitality owed the stranger who knocks at the door. The beloved is forced to wait outside while, obsessed with the poverty of our situation, we try compulsively to find self-seeking remedies. In this regard, you might remember the story of Psyche and Eros. Psyche finds herself self-absorbed after love has suddenly left her to face an apprehensive solitude. Having broken her vow not to behold her beloved, she pities herself. But she is given a chance to repair things. Psyche is summoned to three tests arranged by her mother-in-law, Aphrodite. Unaccustomed to ordeals, she nonetheless succeeds with the help of allies. She breaks out of the closed circle of her ego. Then, in a more open position, she can undertake the preparation necessary to love's work: a sojourn through the land of the dead. Once more at Aphrodite's command, she departs. Succeeding beyond expectation, she is initiated on return into love's labors. She is given in marriage to her beloved Eros

> *The light of splendor shines in the middle of the night.*
> *Who can see it? A heart which has eyes and watches,*

writes Angelus Silenus. That is an apt way to put it. The poet in him likens the font to light's splendor. This clarifies what is asked of the heart. The heart's work lies in watchfulness since to watch is to take in without alteration or embellishment. Remorse, the salt produced in the underworld's upper reaches, clears film from the watchful eye. Before, the film prevented the splendor from entering the retina. Now, a life-giving radiance can enter without obstruction. The heart is similarly guileless in how it loves. It betrays nothing of the beloved's beauty and by beholding it singularly without guile sees it to completion. This is the way the heart remains steadfast throughout the changing rhythms of its beloved.

By now, you know how love's work is to cleanse the heart's eye. Then the heart can feel itself reflected as an image in the basin into which the font pours. Leaning closer, it can, furthermore, encompass the basin, mother-vessel of nutrients for fructification. Cleansing brings about a peace or a resolution of conflict. Opposition belongs to impulsive desire in its native form. The impulse of desire naturally expresses itself simultaneously as a positive and negative force. This means that to each 'I want this' is an 'I don't want this;' to each 'I don't want that' is an 'I want that.' Remember how before work's love can artfully begin, the soul must be prepared. In a work toward refinement and clarity, raw material must enter a process toward these very ends. First, you need to awaken to the dynamic of 'natural' desire. Although a difficult challenge, the effort takes an awareness of two opposing components of one and the same desire—the affirming and the denying—and how they share a mutual attraction. This, above all else: the 'yes' and the 'no,' the male and the female, want to couple.

Recognition of an attractive force between opposites represents an important stage of development. Love is being readied to work. The affirming impulse, the 'I want,' desires to be conjoined with the denying, the 'I don't want' impulse. This may seem to you the natural course of things, it is actually a strange new phenomenon. To find how each desire enfolds its opposite, is really twinned and two-fold, is secret knowledge. I cannot tell you how to come to it, although I have. I can say how it has an unexpected finale, which is this. Attraction, as you know, brings arousal. Arousal leads to consummation. In consummation, desire, having shown its secret double nature, now reveals its true secret. It goes to its death while still in its prime. Then the enigmatic passage to the underworld takes place. Who is it who can undertake the adventure? The old desire that lay in opposition to itself has perished. At its sexual height, conjunction leaves behind nothing of the old. A reconciling passion—the eternal flame of the beloved--has utterly consumed it. Some irrevocably new being emerges from mortification. I will tell you more of its unique identity. For now know it is born with what is alone worth seeking: a heart of incorruptible desire. This incorruptible desire is what we all yearn after, for it is the desire to be loved.

By now, you recognize how birth of an incorruptible heart is the primary work of love. It is where love's work begins and ends. From the ashes of impulse desire that was incinerated under a fierce heat of attraction, a transubstantial desire is born. What do I mean by this? I mean it is akin to a swelling of a love for life. It takes place in the heart. The different substance of transubstantial desire comes from an unknown origin in the land of the dead, much farther than anything on earth, on the way to beyond. Although the new matter is astral, you should not assume that it has been retrieved from below. What comes from below is a catalyst, in the original sense that catabasis. It helps bring the reaction, but itself is unchanged. Its incorruptible heart comes from the way it wishes to return always to its own sphere. There, there would be a starry kind of incorruptibility, how the stars watch us with an eye of eternity. There lies, you know, the overflowing origin. Love's first work is to revisit its original place, there. The essence of the act lies in renewal, for there love can remember itself forever. Overflowing, love can rain upon receptive hearts who walk the earth and rejuvenate itself through their act.

This shows love is a circulation. It moves to regenerate itself in such a way that it never comes to its exhaustion. This proves its home is with the infinite, for any finite act is eventually exhausted and finished. On the contrary, love works to be self-regenerating, never exhausted by movement, always being in movement. You must come to understand the two directions of love that Plato speaks of. One comes from above and costs nothing. It frees up life below from oppressive laws and facilitates a search for the book. Before the second can begin, love needs to descend to the third world, beneath. There, dead material mysteriously bestows new life, life of a new order and sex. Then, the real ascent of love begins, until the son of the philosopher, representative of the Great Work appears. In the reaches of human life, transformation by contact with the stone is strenuously to be sought. By now, you have surmised that you must be a good gardener to cultivate love for the life it brings—to 'grow' a swelled and open heart. That means you also have deduced means for relating the twin streams by means of the representative's sublime power.

Turn to some images of alchemy that I have found helpful. Look first at a remarkable sixteenth century creation, the *Rosarium philosophorum* and confirm just this thought. They show a sequence of ten or eleven images for representing various stages of love's work.

Picture 1
The Mandala Fountain

Picture 2
Emergence of the Opposites

Picture 3
Stripped for Action

Picture 4
Descent into the Bath

Picture 5
Union, Manifestation of the Mystery

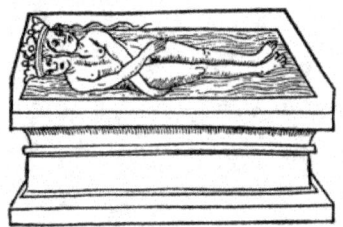

Picture 6
In the Tomb

Picture 7
Separation of Soul and Body

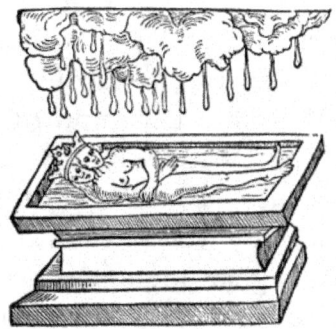

Picture 8
Gideon's Dew Drips from the Cloud

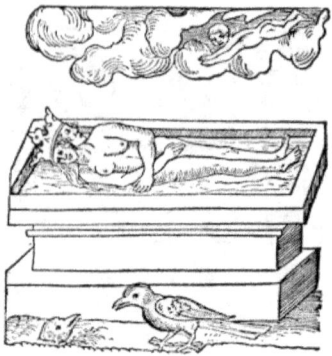

Picture 9
Reunion of Soul and Body

Picture 10
Resurrection of the United Eternal Body

The first five are to apprentice yourself to the work yet do not belong to the work proper. They describe the downward stream I mentioned a moment ago. They show how its action impregnates the impulse of desire with the impulse to be present to itself. Self-conscious desire they is ready for its test, the journey upward. In the *Rosarium*, the last five images show how love actually works. They follow the maturation of a desire as it aspires to its higher origin and remains at the same time incarnate in the body. This event may be realized and if so, the alchemist has a final image. In it, you notice a radical inversion. Desire for love has become love for desire. Feeling loved, desire abandons its petty conflicts and relaxes into being itself. Then, desire comes to know a striving after incorruptibility being for it itself wants to become without corruption, perishing, death. In short, it wants to know what alone is worth seeking, the philosopher's stone.

Take another look at the images. In picture 1, there is an illustration of the fountain of life. From three spigots flow the waters. They represent the trinity of forces that underlie all worlds. The law of three is a basic law. It imputes that all phenomena are composed by three quite separate forces or sexes. The twin serpents, male and female, are entwined in a caduceus, and represent both descending and ascending, or bestowing and gathering, currents of love. A star at the base of each marks where the third force enters from its astral origin. The actual two-fold nature of desire has not yet showed itself. Nor has the possibility of betrayal. Of desire becoming present to itself is only an undreamed dream. The sun and moon can bear it witness, though. The two symbolize the two sexes inherit in human desire formed out respect for opposition. From these two come day and night, light and dark, hot and cold, firm and yielding, offering and receiving. Before they do, and while there remains the *yes* and *no* of desire, there has to be masculine and feminine, here pictured as a king and a queen. These are given sexual identities on the path of transformation. There is no way to progress without encountering them.

Two-fold desire appears in picture 2. Do you note that the two are not mirror images of each other? Narcissus is a story of a young man who learns the hard way that this is so when he falls in love with his own image. When desire is present to itself, it is two-fold. It is present to the contradiction of itself. It yearns to unburden itself. Where does the third, which is of astral origin, come in? It comes in the turn, that quick, silent movement where you look at yourself. Then you see the oppositions living in the other's death, and dying in its live. Masculine and feminine come in there. They come in the look from above that itself is undivided. The look of that look is love. Love looks in on conflict and brings peace. The repellent character of affirming only and never receiving is pacified. Firm balance is created in this fashion. The firmer the balance, the closer the stone becomes. That is an attractive destiny. After much war, with *yes* and *no* averse to each other, nothing can be more fervently wished. The dove's gift becomes highly attractive. For attraction brings a peculiar recognition that you should mark, of a need to be loved by the other.

That marks the start of a willingness to be obedient. The event is sure to be auspicious.

The net effect of attraction appears in picture 3. Under influence of the dove's beneficence, we see the nude bathers. Their garments symbolizing firm and yielding, masculine and feminine, have been taken off. Each appears without adornments, just as it is, desirous and desired. This is the timeless spell of desire. It awakens in the oldest recollection a primordial urge for union. For Plato, Aristophanes gives a light-hearted account of the mystery that you must hear about. According to it, humans were once large, spherical, double-sexed beings. With four arms and four legs, they seemed too powerful for the gods, who feared them. But they feared them mostly because the beings could satisfy their own desire. So the gods split them in two. That memory buried deep within us drives them also to want to reunite with the opposite sex. We are roused from sleep and indifference to seek that partner in climax. In Picture 3, that is in the future. They there are still commemorating a desire for a wedding. If we read the captives, the solar king says, 'O Luna, let me be thee husband.' The lunar queen replies, 'O Sol, I must submit to thee.' But you must not overlook the dove's words, because two can never make a child. The dove reminds us of that. 'The spirit is what vivifies,' he says.

When you come to attraction, celebrated in picture 4, look at the ritual bath as a baptismal font. In it, masculine is coupled with feminine in a representation of impulsive desire. The image is a bit more complicated than that. The bath is used for a special cleansing in which the named are relieved of their names. In these waters, they revert to primordial identities in which the other 'half' finds the one desired and desirable. They return to a dynamic in which a simple *yes* desires a *no* and vice versa. You could say that they are more deeply immersed in the waters of life and its absolving effect. Immersion permits a fuller, more fluid contact of each with the other, and this is symbolized by the three streams that flow from the font. The dove's presence is also significant. The dove, by attesting to the crescendo of attraction, provides a calming witness from the starry realm. Any conflict in desire is soothed by its presence while both parties are reminded of their higher purpose. An urge toward a state without opposition builds. This is a new desire that would persist even after conjunction was complete and over. It is a quixotic desire that I have alluded to. It embodies a transcendent awareness, that is, awareness of love's destiny. It is an awareness that renders the coupling sacred but that never enters into the act. Is there not an incorruptible absence here?

Picture 5 is pivotal because it signifies the end of the preparatory sequence and beginning of love's work proper. It looks both ways because it is the last of two-fold desire, both affirming and submitting, and the first of contact and penetration. You see how astral guidance is no longer visible because the couple is entombed, that is, somewhere below ground. At this enigmatic stage, love's work is depicted by the specifics of conjunction: masculine above, feminine below. It represents a correct alignment of desires insofar as it furthers the destiny of conjunction. How is love's destiny advanced? An affirming desire must enter into the sphere of a submissive one, which in turn must receive and engulf it. An active desire must meet a passive one and remain without withdrawing. If alignment is correct and the time not hurried, what Diotima calls the greater mystery ensues. You may know it as the mystery of exchange. Finer matter blends with coarser, the one interpenetrates the other. The mixing is at the same time an impregnation. It takes place, moreover, under the auspices of an invisible third, the dove that has absconded. How could this be an ordinary pregnancy? To the darkened dove of non-being, both donor and recipient give up their respective claims to existence. They respect the absolute emptiness of the tomb. They honor the superior power that brings them together with its dead stillness. They lie there, waiting without expectation.

In picture 6, we are given a glimpse into the aftermath of impulsive desire, torn between 'I want' and 'I don't want' that retain their separate identities. The two are at last conjoined, but lo and behold, they have died. Can you follow the event that you are witnessing? Death has occurred, but what kind? Of whom or what? Whose identity is now given to walk the land of the dead and with what task to fulfill? Before this picture, there were two desiring entities, one positive, one negative. Now only one remains, an amalgam of the two. This one remains entombed. Apparently, a death has overtaken the 'I' who wanted and the 'I' who didn't, and now momentarily restrains the fused being. What is represented in the image of fusion? Before, both desires were identified with or 'corrupted by' what they wanted. The object of desire mixed with and tainted the character of the impulse. The taint affected the essence of impulsive desire. The taint made it necessary for the impulse to die if a purity of desire was ever to be regained. For desire lost its mark and began to err as soon as it grew forgetful. Made to serve as love's awakening, desire became self-serving. It started to love itself, like Narcissus in the story. Split in two by the fascination, it grew unmindful of its purpose and outlived its usefulness. Will the new amalgam, the androgyne, be any different? We do not yet know since it has yet to acquire a living identity. It is not dead any more than a seed is. It has a kind of weight, as Dante had when he stepped into the ferry to cross the River Styx. In reality, however, we did not know since the future being lies in a crypt, which is an odd womb, if it is that. When we ask, what is to be born, an even stranger answer comes. We await the birth of desire indivisible, a desire without resistance, hesitation, avidity, incivility, or impropriety. Or more properly, we await its rebirth, since desire of that metal once poured with love from the source. If such a birth should occur, it would take place in the heart, since the very conception of desire, is one that remembers the heart of the matter. In any event, the seed, in the heart of the tomb, lies before your eyes. Inspect it for it contains a germ of new life. Let the eye of your heart take it in, for there, love is at work. It is already at work, striving to germinate life and a love of the same.

I have taken you to the end of a preparatory effort. This is all I can say of the series up to now. There is much more to be said about picture 6, but since it concerns love's work proper, I want to defer telling you. It would move to the allusion of conscience, which can be another chapter. Nonetheless, a summary of the remaining pictures might be helpful to you at this point. Look again at picture 6, where you see the tomb of the androgyne that appears to be dead. What does the state signify? To the ancients, it is a way of denoting to the heart's desire. The heart desires to breathe in the atmosphere of love and be open to what is. In this respect, it is informed by a single and singular event: the feeling of the underworld. That feeling is etched in the silence of the tomb. We can know about it from those who made the most thorough study of it, the

Egyptians. They knew so much that they inscribed instructions for transformation on the stone walls of their funerarial vaults. In the tomb, the entombed heart could grasp the silence in a special manner, for it is indeed the most exquisite of silences, silence squared. It is a quiet unto death. It therefore traverses the interstices between the living and the dead, and wraps its blessed shroud over both. Coming to life in the tomb, we can ascertain the quiet that is in the constant background to life's emphatic sound. Our entire life passes against the backdrop of dead silence. In the tomb, free from distraction, the androgyne comes to a unity to which both life and dead silence belong and feels the aloneness as itself.

Conscience forms in the dark. Can you see that in the image of picture 7? The dark is the tomb that the ancients respect. They felt the dead dark of burial sites could be penetrated only by special solar or stellar events like a solstice or the rising Dog Star. Otherwise, the dark was needed in order that consciousness form in tombs. Entombed, when pulse and heartbeat fade into an abysmal background, one begins to feel oneself. In that aloneness that alone initiates desire into the ways of love, one feels what it is like being without qualities. It is a pure life-force to which qualities get added on later. But, you ask, what feels being? What is there when the luminosity is turned so low? If I could call it an organ, I would say the heart is what feels when there is nothing to feel but that. The heart is a creature of the dark, and through its feel conscience appears. Conscience is the name of the heart's feeling. Conscience *is* the feeling heart, the heart of feeling. Conscience, in the name of feeling, brings the rest of life's love to awakening. How is it possible that the names of all other things are spoken when there is only silence? Think of conscience being 'secreted' like a vapor or atmosphere. This is the idea of picture 7 that shows an image of a cloud bearing the label of an infant. This gives proof of how conscience is the vaporization of the androgynous corpse as it lies in dead silence. The cloud is fertile with droplets of all things to be.

The cloud of conscience grows so heavy with atmosphere that it precipitates. You, the alchemist, must imagine how a supersaturated solution can precipitate out a salt. The liquor grows pregnant with seeds that must, at a certain point, be dropped. In this image, think of conscience that is salt. Specifically, it is born of sublimated mercury and sulfur, male and female. The precipitate is the subject of picture 8. Conscience rains on the dead body of desire. It is feeling which, like water, evaporated into thin air. It condensed around dust particles, 'impurities,' and formed gray, swirling clouds. The empty tomb has become full with various formations. At critical point, it rains, a fertile rain. Rain falls in drops from the cloud. The cycle of conscience is completed and life returns to the arid tomb. Beyond what I have told you, the composition of that life remains unknown, a mystery. From a coupling dark and entombed, life springs forth, fecundated by knowledge of the dead.

A fertilized seed, the young shoot splits open the hard, dead pod. This is life's basic act. Feeling bubbles forth from the entombed heart. It has been initiated into the relation between life and its background of the non-living. Because life constantly changes, the core-awareness also is in constant flux. Like the heart, it continually fluctuates. The core, however, is not merely that life is greater since it possesses an awareness that surpasses life. Since it is an awareness surpassing life, it derives from elsewhere than life. To that place, if it is that, we have no direct access. But there are sidelong glimpses, the more heart-feeling, the more penetrating they are. Light accumulates so that at some point, a change occurs. Perhaps I should say that it had taken place earlier without giving any notice. Nonetheless now, it is obvious that the tomb is open to the sky. Picture 9 shows the shift by drawing our attention to two birds standing by the side of the tomb. The ravens of mortification have returned to the radiance of the sun! One is not fully unburied. Also, there is an even more hopeful change taking place. The vaporous cloud of conscience now descends toward the entombed being. The vital meaning of the event is symbolized by the emblem of an infant child flying downward. Once it arrives, it will revivify the body with an unaccustomed joy of life. It will restore a sense of love's destiny, sought in the long sojourn through the low lands of the dead. It will bring life not subject to impulse of desire, nor its amnesia regarding love. Moving beyond sorrow's heavy memory, the new life will be buoyant enough to imitate that love that lets life be. This already is a draught of the elixir of incorruptibility. Do you not feel the thirst rising in you to drink deeply or drink not at all?

CONSCIENCE

The lover, a true philosopher who loves truth's light, undertakes an extraordinary underground journey. The aim, you must know, is knowledge of intelligible things, things of the astral realm, which cannot be found by a living light. Before nourishing a desire for life on earth, life's opposite must be met and understood. One must walk the land of the dead as one *in* it, but not *of* it. Direct rays of the sun and stars cannot find entry into a heart that opens inwardly. The lover must awaken to the downward path, die to a life that fears it, and be reborn as a new consciousness. An ever-new consciousness, the heart, is pregnant with what is found neither in life or its perennial backdrop, death, but surpasses both. I am speaking of what gleams once the infernal regions are behind you. It is the cold light of conscience, the incorruptible heart. It has a feel all its own, like the composure of being. This is the composure to watch like that of a stone. For this reason, conscience has always been called the 'philosopher's stone.'

Conscience, I said, is formed by the dark of the tomb. In the tomb, nothing moves. Quiet reigns, the quiet of the dead. The quiet signifies an absence, an absence of the pulse. Alien to life, the quiet is prefigured by the stranger whose origin and purpose are unknown and who appears quietly 'across a crowded room.' Immersion in the tomb's quiet—that special baptism—is conveyed by the sojourn through the world below. There, the sojourner repeatedly meets life's absence in a variety of ways. We can look to lore to verify how this happens. When he is in Hades, Odysseus notices a lack of color and solidity in the dead souls. Dante's vision is more psychologically acute since he notes their lack of will and determination. In the inferno, whatever the souls do is limited to compulsive repetition. So, too, in the tomb, we can expect that as the lover comprehends more and more quiet, particles of conscience condense and precipitate onto the open heart. Up to that point, the heart is parched and arid. Then, after the rainfall, the heart becomes verdant and sentient. Being sentient, it exhibits the signature of conscience: it knows itself as creature and created.

Think back to the *Rosarium* pictures in the last chapter. Rain, whose power it is to open the heart, pours down from a heavy cloud. Vapor has been formed from the 'sublimation' of desire, and now, what goes up must fall down. If you look closely, in the dark recess of the tomb, the lover experiences remorse. This is strange, but she feels penitent because she lacks real desire. She is dead for this reason. All desire in her is divided and has two voices, one that says *yes* and one *no* when in the face of the thing desired. Yet, love, she surmises, relates to a different desire. The difference is that it neither affirms nor denies, nor both, but is passionately other in its make-up. Knowing just this much and deprived of real desire, the lover is filled with remorse. She wants to love but cannot. Bitter tears of salt run down her cheeks, evaporate, rise, and accumulate in the atmosphere. Through sufficient weeping, the dew-point is reached. Then the rains begin in the tomb.

What is the strange rain that softly falls in the dark tomb? It is none other than the water of life. The fountain from which it overflows represents the primordial condition of picture 1 in the *Rosarium* sequence.

Picture 1
The Mandala Fountain

The fool, who is the absolute zero of consciousness, intuits it directly. Because the knowledge is visceral, it remains inarticulate and inexpressible and a fool's words suffer their ineffability. They fall on deaf ears, save the stranger's who alone understands the fool's situation. But because the stranger lives at the margin, no one believes the stranger's story. Its strangeness is taken to be a rebellious distrust and lore on the font itself grows fantastic, the stuff of fairy tales. Its point is lost. In order to retrieve the meaning, the lover agrees to an impossible quest. It is to set the world aright. Once, the font showed its abundance for all to see, now, because of our incredulity, its munificence is reserved for a closed and vaulted tomb. This is the fact of our 'fallen' condition.

You should remember that everything depends on an entombment of quiet. The font's resurgence cannot occur amidst the clash of opposites, where the 'I want' seeks to destroy the 'I don't want.' In the sublunary world, desire is divided and speaks with deep ambiguity. Every desire is at war with itself. Yet in war, adversaries attract, as did Romeo and Juliet of the play. A display of attraction, lure and counter-lure, harbors a possibility but also full of distraction. This is life's dance, king and queen together, and the making of a grand show of beauty. Isn't there beauty wherever love is born? Beauty is there from the first acknowledgement of attraction to the revealing nakedness of the 'ritual bath.' Its presence gathers. In the end, you will agree with Plato that love appears the day of beauty's wedding. Yet unless male and female, active and passive, relate to themselves rightly, their courtship will be in vain. In this connection, you must try to bear in mind an important law: intercourse requires participation of equals. Unequals cannot join together. It further must seclude itself in an enclosed place, a 'sealed flask,' far away from terrestrial influences. There, it will develop a sensitivity to an invisible astral radiance that penetrates all life. When these conditions are met, something wonderful happens. The conjunction of opposites invites the mysterious third force. It brings both male and female to their death and from the breath of their decomposition, the tomb fills with a primordial cloud. Once again beginning, the fountain overflows, this time with dark, generous spring rain. This event has been anticipated for all of time since it nourishes an incorruptible desire for life.

The rain of entombment differs in an important way from the original waters. From the font, innocence streams. Life is neither good nor bad but is simply, without qualities. In the hero's descent through the land of the dead, however, when rain comes, it is ablution. Ablution denotes a cleansing wash. The absolving power of water is prefigured in picture 4 of the *Rosarium* sequence. There, the 'I want' and the 'I don't want,' king and queen, bathe together in a basin below the fountain. Earthly desire, in its intrigue of opposition, is being purified of its morbidity. The hero's adventure calls for another kind of absolution. In the tomb, in order to give over completely to the way of death, the hero needs an ablution of life. The holy rain must remove all vitality from the once-living body. Only then can the heart opened and its matter impregnated by conscience.

By then, the hero has become other than himself. He is hero because he sets out to battle the warring desires. Now, passing through the underworld and 'defeating' desires, he is remade. Now whole, he is a philosopher qualified to bear the stone. Or, as said in ancient times, he is son of the philosophers. Newly made, a new Adam or the risen Christ, he reminds us of the thither side of heroism. It is another image that he recalls. The image of Jesus harrowing the fields of hell conveys the heart's pregnancy with conscience. That Jesus uses an instrument of fertility, the plow, on the soil of death symbolizes an enigmatic occurrence. The image is of readying spent, lifeless matter for sowing. What can possible grow in ash? His act is in preparation for a life-form beyond any that we know. It is a form not subject to the laws of terrestrial decay.

Harrowing the fields of hell represents an act of transcendent fertility. Jesus is the gardener who goes beyond heroism to bring life forth from its opposite. He also is the philosopher who knows to sow gold in 'white foliated earth.' The science of using ash to grow things in derives from the fundamental experience of the tomb. There, we saw, the hero feels the being of the self. At the same time, at the heart of the matter, he feels being without qualities, non-being. This poses the ultimate and final conjunction Knowledge that lies beyond living and dying, new knowledge, is Jesus' special province. There, the spirit whose source lies in the starry world soars. To sow seeds of life in the fields of death is to borrow the pregnancy of the image and embody it in the being who was once hero. Hero no longer, he is, as depicted by an additional picture specific to the *Rosarium* sequence, the Christ resurrected.

Jesus is hero of conscience. His science directs the lover to grow naked in desire and not resist attraction to the opposing desire. It guides the lover's quest for the beloved, which is an unequivocal love for providence. It encourages the lover. Even when walking through the valley of the shadow of death, she fears no evil. There, she knows a life-renewing remorse for not being acceptant. Her way is a pool of tears and two eyes wet with weeping. When at the far reach of the underworld, a revivifying rain falls, the science encourages her to rise up and take new life. His science is a geography of the dead and an anatomy of suffering. It is a science of the second baptism. While the first baptism (as in picture 4) is by water, the second is by fire. His science teaches the passage through the fire of mortification.

Mortification is a dark fire. It is the fire of the tomb where the absolute and absolving quiet has burned away all dross. Dross represents the conflicted nature of our ordinary desires. Because we both want and don't want a thing, a certain quivering takes place within us. There is a back-and-forth movement as we resolve and then unresolve to get what we are after. Because the motive is mixed, the object is never whole-heartedly sought. We are, to a degree, passive as we go after it. Our impulse is impure, neither fully affirming nor denying. We cannot, furthermore, correct the situation by a mere effort of will. No matter how much we really want something, the nature of desire remains the same, that is, conflicted. Only a change in the identity of who desires makes a difference. That change requires a dark fire.

Salt provides the dark fire of a second baptism. The first baptism, by water, concerns the body with its fleshy, organic substance. As Nicodemus learns from Jesus, it is essential to immense the body in the waters of life so that one will become attached to the earth, its beauties and tribulations. Otherwise, what is offered may be rejected, and a malaise setting in. Here, the refusal may bring an urge for a premature leaves-taking, with the wastage that that implies. By contrast, the second baptism, by fire, is an immersion of the 'second' body. It differs radically from the first baptism. Baptism by water names and celebrates but does not create the terrestrial body. But baptism by fire is a creative act. The action of salt, from tears of remorse, makes the substance of a new body. The substance of the second body is produced by smelting that of the old fleshy body. Purified by immersion in salt, the 'transubstantiated' being has different properties from the body of earth. It obeys different laws, those of the astral region.

We feel fire the moment when salt is poured on an open wound. There is burning in how it cleanses the tissue of infection and attacks the cause. Pain comes as a verification of saline action. Salt works within by analogy. Through heat, desire is purged of the contention between the *yes* with the *no*. Salt combusts the two, transforms their substance, and vaporizes it to form an atmosphere of desire. This desire is a new kind and it begins to gather above like a fragrant smoke. This is because is has borne the heat of tears' salt similar to how wood bears fire's. In both cases, a dead ash is left after the gases expelled from life rise. But in salt's case, combustion also means oxygen prepared for the new body as it lifts toward the stars. Where does its durability come from? As it was reduced to ash, salt was also preparing the metal to contain the substance. Could it have prepared it for joining with an independent existence, the second body, as it lives just inside the first?

The physics of fire brings about manifest change. In this, fire of all kinds shares in its material property with the stars and their thermonuclear combustion. In each and every spark, there is a seed of hydrogen fusion, or some even more immense energy. Between the two is a series of leaps. Each leap, each discontinuity, represents a trial of remorse. There are tears and weeping that let salt accumulate. It is an action that opens the terrestrial body, wracked as it is with inner conflict, to another force. Its oxidizing effect intensifies the *yes* against the *no* that calls upon a new force to appear. Each leap, therefore, is unpredictable in its appearance though with appearance comes quantum change. Cell by cell, another element is secreted. There is life in it and more life the longer it gathers. That is how you see fire work.

A period of remorse ends when a veil abruptly lifts. That signals the onset of something new. You see how the fire is put out and the salt's action terminates. Overall, you are left with a feeling of having paid for something even if you don't know what. But you know how payment is not a retribution that has been exacted to atone for past errors. Remorse is not a kind of regret, which is an emotion colored by nostalgia. Instead, you need to remember how remorse pays 'in advance.' It has been referred to as a deposit against future debts and it is surely at least a little like that. You like to think it will bring the golden bird of transformation. In the image of a phoenix that rises from the flames of immolation, all you know is the life being left. Remorse is similar in the way that it looks back. The fire is in order to immolate impurities of the eye toward our inner, incorruptible nature. Of that nature, it needs do nothing. Seeing that is perfection. Purification involves more periods of remorse. It is after each atonement that we face more and more the indestructible core that we that face us. And grow infinite in the difference.

***

Reflect on what happens after conjunction is past. Do you have an image of how the partners remain locked in a hermaphroditic embrace? This powerful symbol relates directly to conscience. It is a sublimation, in the alchemical sense of the word, of the joining. It shows how, after heat passes, conscience can rise to heaven and beyond on the released energy, even unto the star realm. For most purposes, it is imperative to feel how conscience rises, a cloud of atonement, a being-at-one with oneself. As a cloud, its home is in the atmosphere. But even there, it knows its true origin lies higher, which is where it constantly seeks to go. If you could look more deeply into the hermaphroditic mind, you would see the dream of just that. Or you could say that mind is a child of the dream, its mother.

Plato once had an important question. If a true philosopher loves only the sight of the truth, he asked, than why does he eventually go back to the cave? It contains a corruptible vision of things. If the philosopher earns a conscience by his own labors, why would he risk its loss in returning? This is a hard one to answer. But you must know how as conscience grows, it grows increasingly aware of its origin. There, at its source, it holds on to nothing. It completely owns its freedom. Holding to nothing, you exclude nothing, not even the dark cave, the tomb, and the non-dwelling. The fact is that if a true philosopher resists a return to dimness, he is not yet free. He has only followed the call of his vocation, lover of wisdom, up to a degree. The descent is the final exam. Only those who take it with passion succeed in passing.

The lover knows how much is lacking in the grade and won't make it. Would you call that love's primary cause of suffering? Wisdom is a beloved who must return home, the own place. The lover seeks wisdom, which would be at home, and this is a struggle with himself. To succeed, the lover must wield conflicting forces so that they form a finer harmony.

But you must be careful here. Wisdom is not the result of any struggle but comes entirely on its own. It comes in its own time, at its own place. The road to wisdom lies along the road of sacrifice. Along this, the fire of struggle does its work. The metal is tempered and annealed. In the end, though, you come to wisdom only when it comes to you, and struggle is over. You feel there is nothing to struggle with. In the ecstasy, everything is given. You need only to receive, and conscience will be empowered. There is a harmonization. Conscience is wisdom's not opposing life but living in accordance with it. It sees a rightness in every situation. That is the outermost signature of love's work and a most positive indication.

Wisdom is intuitive. It does not think back on something which can then be brought up for future discussion. Conscience lets the lover be aligned with a situation. It makes it possible to meet the demands. It dictates how to act in accordance with what is demanded. It is up to you not to stand in the way of what happens because that is what responsibility is. Responsibility means, to stay with the heart. The heart of a lover, is a listening heart — that is its wisdom. Whenever it listens, it listens to what wisdom has to say. 'The heart has its reasons that the mind will never know.' It grasps things directly, by their essence, not by their attributes.

The rightness conscience writes into each and every situation is felt as harmony. You should be attentive to this. The more you look, the more you find it everywhere. That should be enough to verify how the font's waters overflow everything. They stream down on you each moment. Being eternal, they vary but little. It is our perception of their source that undergoes constant change. Sometimes conscience can be more responsive, sometimes less. In any case, the lover begins to find a special sensitivity awareness. In the awareness, you can see the gold given by a stream of golden waters. That is a touch of the philosopher's stone.

Rumi writes a poem about the event. I want to remember it to you. It goes thus:

When the kernel swells the walnut shell
or the pistachio or the almond, the husk diminishes.
As the kernel of knowledge grows,

The Shock of Love

the husk thins and disappears
because the lover is consumed by the beloved.

The swelling kernel swells with incorruptible desire. Desire that is incorruptible no longer has anything to do with death. It remains completely indifferent to what happens after gratification. In this way, desire lives in a state of desiring. Desire lives on and on, ever fresh in its non-fulfillment. It enlarges and gathers strength. In its perfection, desire is not hobbled by any internal conflicts. You have freed it from an impulse to attain its end, and now desire desires to become for love. Love has been waiting and is forever open to desire. Plato reminds us how love is hungry since it is born of need. Love has been waiting forever for desire to run with lips open to the wind for it, love. Now, desire is hungry for food. It is starved for life. It needs to *feel* the heart's hunger and be at the center. There, the heart has joined in as lover and beloved join. Desire's awakening to love is a great event, long awaited. For now the lover has arrived at the point of being consumed by infinite love.

That point when a lover is consumed by his beloved, do not think that the food of life has sated the appetite. This is not true, not even for a moment. Wisdom, omnipresent and unperceived, comes not to slake desire but to rouse its hunger. Even after her advent, wisdom does not bring satisfaction since she is ungraspable. She is smoke or vapor, cloud or mist. You breathe her in and out but she never remains. If it were otherwise, wisdom would become potential material for a conflict. That is the way of the world. In emptiness, wisdom has an incorruptibility that true desire alone seeks. Wisdom is the voice of God that rings in the ear without saying a single word. She reminds us that love is not more substantial than an echo, and as enduring. To try to hold on to it is to prevent hearing its recurrence. Wisdom enters, a presence that appears when love is inviting. Her luster is the present moment's shimmer as it glows with actuality. A true lover avoids the mistakes of Psyche and Orpheus in the stories and accepts it at face value, not needing to know the identity of the beloved. A true lover embodies wisdom in a desire for the complete penetration of the beloved. He does not know or care what other gifts may come so long as gratitude is felt in the presence to the enigma. In the annihilation of identity, the lover feels gladness. For, in that death comes the food that the beloved provides, and the assurance for a new life.

PRESENCE

Awaken, die, be reborn. Attraction, conjunction, resurrection. These are the major stages of desire. In the later stages, after everything has been paid for and debt wiped out, the finer separates from the coarser on its own. You see how it rises in a cloud and becomes another element, air. Earth plus fire equals air. The transformation is governed by a principle I have given you: the ethereal rises by nature to the stars, showing its astral origin. Matter of the proper composition has its source beyond the earth. As you move toward a fineness, you discover how the astral is the first 'condensation' of the material world. Before that, desire is 'pure' and life but a stirring in its bosom. Regardless of its object, all earthly desire aspires to its origin, which, as the word tells us, is in the stars. It desires a refinement of its nature. In its coarse state, it suffers conflict and sees things in terms of opposites. As a finer perception develops, desire moves beyond properties and qualities, into that without qualities. Here, it drinks from a spring which sustains the created world. Here is the well that waters creation. From here alone flows what can rouse a thirst for life that can never be slaked. This is what desire in its heart of hearts alone seeks.

You need to bear in mind how what I call presence is really remembering. It is not accurate to say that it is life that is remembered. Life is what comes from the act of remembrance but is not there to start. This is the paradox that life is given but must be paid for. The beloved is there but leaves unless the lover invites her in. A lover must first learn to open and in that there is payment. You must be quite clear on the matter. Otherwise, nostalgia and indifference will win out. You must recognize that there is a special impulse to begin with. Without it, nothing is possible. In the schools of poetry, the image of a bell, book, or candle was used to refer to the missing element. However it is signified, the lover knows what role to play with respect to it. It is the role of patient witness, for to watch with an alert intelligence for the impulse's onset is the essence of love. How it begins is immaterial since comings and goings differ. A lover's intention to watch and maintain the vigil fills out his duty in the matter. He becomes derelict in it if sleep conquers his watch. This lover is then a poor lover.

The lover's vigilance embodies a philosophy that is based on a subtle impulse. It is the impulse to host or be one. The impulse is subtle because it is embryonic. It is at a very early stage of development, weak and not self-sustaining. Obviously it needs to be nourished. This is where you come in, but it is no easy matter. Do you know whom or what you are inviting in? Of course not. How could you. Look at how portentously the situation is pictured in the drawings: it is a grave watch. You are attending an extended wake, but why? The specific watch kept in the dark silence of the tomb is one you need be acquainted with. Ezra Pound's words are luminous when he speak of the presence in 'The Tomb at Akr Caar':

'I am thy soul, Nikoptis. I have watched
these five millennia, and thy dead eyes
moved not, nor ever answer my desire.

The Egyptian soul keeps watch for eternity. The still, unmoving body belongs to the beloved who waits for its invitation. The beloved watches over a place empty of life. There is no pulse, wind, or nerve of feeling. Yet the beloved-soul watches for signs of an impulse to host. She watches for a message from the living and still absent lover. She watches for a word begin. She is attentive to the faintest first stirring. This is a description of presence for you to digest.

In the tomb of the drawings also, you wait attentively for the return of the absent other. The other, the lover, has gone into the desert. It is a dangerous sojourn and there is no guarantee of a safe return. Nonetheless, the beloved acts as sentry, guarding the gate. Ever-awaiting a gesture of hospitality, gatekeeper faces the direction of opening. It is a beacon to the other to return and enter. The lover is beckoned to enter and return. This is how wisdom sees it. From a true lover's point of view, however, the return is the other way around. It faces an opening to infinity, beyond borders, limits, doorways, or forms. It requires an 'organ' of perception toward infinite, and this organ must have the right feeling for the job. Such an organ is a heart of a true lover. It invites the faceless face of wisdom to penetrate it, and survives on its faith in love alone. What the beloved's wisdom will bring as it enters a true lover's heart is unknown until the moment. To find the impulse to face the unknown is the lover's task. Only perfect love casteth out the fear of wisdom, and it is this that the lover sees in each and every thing he beholds.

Presence consists in a memory of the special impulse. You may know this simply as initiative. It is an initial stroke, an impulse to begin, or an initiation. Its specificity makes it special since without it, there is no beginning is all. Until the beginning, the paradox is that there is no lover who waits timelessly for the unnamed one, the beloved. There can be no wisdom to lighten the world without the impulse to embody wisdom. Since the most ancient of times, presence has been called the herald of wisdom. It is the royal falcon that guards wisdom's coming so carefully that only a true lover is aware. You see how the lover is host of infinity and must provide a vessel to contain the infinitesimal substance of which wisdom is made. I am providing you with such a vessel, in this case, a book of presence. Reading it is a practice and you will uncover the impulse of which I speak. A book of love is a mere preparation, as divine Plato tells, but when he goes on to speak of death, we must understand him more carefully. He means to refer to the watch in the tomb. For there, your heart opens unto death and knows the life divine. For there, your desire gains incorruptibility. Then, you find how its guardian has been there the whole time, an awareness of a special impulse, unfelt until the present.

The hero of presence is Orpheus. Orpheus has kept his guard over the vow not to look back toward his beloved Eurydice. Think of the inconceivable difficulty. At each moment, he must remember he avowed the impossible. He must neutralize impulses that would ruin him. He must postpone betrayal. It may arise from numerous sources, often ones least expected. His arc of watchfulness is an ascent because as fulfillment nears and the earth opens to his beloved, the urge to ignore his oath likewise strengthens. An intense determination mounts as the end nears. His presence radiates concern for the life-giving impulse. It alone looks future-ward, toward what is to come to pass. But the task is impossible, even for a hero of Orpheus' metal. At a critical moment, he forgets who he is and what is required. Looking around, he turns his back on his obligation. In the same instant, his beloved vanishes forever. The single second in which he abandoned the impulse causes his presence — to her, to wisdom — to blink out. Then he is a hero wracked by remorse too bitter ever to bear fruit.

What do you remember about the impulse of initiative? Recall how male and female. king and queen of the drawings, are fixed after coupling. They are shown lying on their backs in a strange position. It is as though they are merged physically. They stare, not impassioned, but patient as if awaiting an event. The impulse arrives when it does. With it comes a clear awareness. They have the presence to guard it, for it is invaluable. With it, an opening may be searched for and the ongoing flow let in. To the extraordinary place of conjunction, the flow brings a sense of the infinite. Infinite is the source from which wisdom flows. Now, name, if you can, the impulse of presence. If you know, it would be called *desire*. Desire is desirous to love and to let wisdom make its entry. Desire guards against reticence. You cannot be reticent in the face of desire since it urges you strongly to invite life in. The hermaphrodite of the drawings waits expectantly in its tomb for the return of its beloved, and it waits with ever-deepening desire.

Presence, I told you, consists of a unique memory. It remembers how the beginning goes. With everything, there is a beginning. To remember the beginning of each thing is to remember how to begin. Do you? By now, you should know about the stream overflowing and becoming the source of life. Love is just that great abundance. Learn to desire that and that alone. Recognize the power of remembrance, like the Greeks of an earlier time. They made her a great goddess in whose charge the days and years began. The nine Muses came after Zeus left her. Her greatness lies in how she drinks of the current but does not keep track. She is pure desire, made in time's image. Because of her, what passes comes and is past. She fixes it once it has finished becoming. That is her skill.

If you think of it, that unique memory was there with Eurydice when Orpheus turned to look back. It bore her off as she disappeared from the living and whisked to the land of the dead. She becomes memory that can call presence forth. For Orpheus, you will see, she has that power. A memory of her stirs a presence and she appears as living among the dead. In memory, that moment, she is neither alive nor dead. Presence remembers that time and holds that does not go off like an arrow. It is wary of time's changeful face and how it remains ever-fresh, ever-moving. It is on the lookout for evidence of a hidden impulse. That one, it knows, will permit it to maintain an incorruptibility of purpose. In the vessel that holds the quicksilver memory, there is the substance from which to pour your metal. It will provide a pure identity.

Like a metallic vapor, presence rises from the crucible of the heart. There, the moribund being of the drawings lies. You can think present awareness is there as a seed, but your eyes tell a different story. Cold desire lies at the bottom, ash or scum. Almost visible is the most primitive tropism that draws it toward the stars. If you could see the fundamental trajectory of desire, you would see the full upward ascent, the backward movement that completes the circle of creation. Desire is the ore of presence. You must think of the image that the word contains. There is a cold 'heat' of starlight that stirs the ashes—and a cloud of presence rises. Perhaps it had secretly attended the living body all its days but only after an enigmatic death does it gain independence. That is what the poet says:

> *I have been intimate with thee, known thy ways.*
> *Have I not touched thy palms and finger-tips,*
> *Flowed in, and through thee and about thy heels?*

A living cloud hides the impulse. It is the 'word of God' hidden by the cloud. In itself, it is durable as stone, though its endurance is work, unlike the stone's. For the cloud has no stability, and its continuation must be obtained, given the circumstances. Your awareness will waver time and time again. The word of God is spoken in the desert, without ears to hear, and persists unwavering. Listen for its beacon. Occasionally, you will catch a whisper and after a number of them, conscience awakens. This is the great event. It is a new beginning, a resurrection. Remember what a teacher of conscience once said. 'Fortunate is one who stands at the beginning. That one will know the end and will not taste death.' Hold your mouth up to the sky and drink in the rain.

In the image of a cloud, there is a special emphasis on presence. If you follow, you will next imagine a veil. Why a veil? Because it obscures what it contains and preserves it by obscurity. It is analogous to a vapor from ground heading to some upper region. And so it is with the breath, the vaporous veil of the living. In breath you find movement. In your very first study of the breath, see how it forms and disappears. Where does it go once it defies and crosses all borders? That place is veiled so we have only the fluctuation to follow. Yet, that is enough since it is the nature of the heart to fluctuate. The heart, a physical pump, expands and contracts—systole and diastole. Life follows analogous patterns of respiration and circulation. The feel, likewise, obeys patterns similar to those of cloud. Touch the waves and it is already gone. This poses a real problem for you. Contact with presence is extremely evanescent and that is in the nature of contact. At the same time, you are faced with a vow of vigilance. How do you get through this dilemma? Orpheus in his wisdom can help. If you follow, Rilke will get you to the crux of the matter:

> *O how he has to vanish, for you to grasp it!*
> *Though he himself take fright at vanishing.*
> *Even while his word transcends the being-here,*
> *he's there already where you do not follow.*

The character of the cloud is in sympathy the stranger's. Besides, both are early harbinger of love's desire. To see what I mean, recall how on a clear day, a cloud is stranger to the sky. It can look alien or even an intruder. The cloud and the stranger share a peculiar relation with light. Both cast a shadow and do not let you see their far side. That air of mystery is not broken when a breath-taking sunset cloud reminds how the shadow-making serves. Light's glory is more emphatic with it. To continue my string of analogy, the cloud of presence bears a resemblance to the stranger. Both remind desire of the other to what desire naturally seeks. Presence disrupts the impulsive basis of desire. In the disruption, there is an opportunity to catch sight of the font overflowing. It is clouded there, in front of your eyes that are nervous in front of it. You are afraid you will lose what you were striving to achieve. You fear how things will turn to ash under its shadowed light. Nonetheless, love reminds you to look beyond. Does the cloud contain a rain meant to vivify life? At this point, you lack no answer. You know how in its dew, desire needs no urge for its high mission. You yourself can recall its origin. Memory of that begins life to vibrate at a higher pitch. The new substance is like that.

Analogously, a cloud is womb for the rain and presence for another body. A cloud offers protection so an embryo can grow in power and strength. The embryo is the body of the beginning. At its heart, human presence guards an enigmatic impulse to begin. Its incarnation consists in the embryo about which I speak. Your task is to nurture 'prenatal development.' Be careful enough to maintain a connection to the source. That way, you will be supplied with nutrients for the second body. Because the body, organs and tissues, are composed of elements from above, the second body's nature will be different from your first one that contains the impulses of desire. The second one is celestial and star-like. The desire that moves it — love in its purest form — is the gold at the end of the work I describe. You need to watch for it in your action and thought.

What does the inner body exist for? The riddle, an early one, dates back to antiquity. In one rendition, *you* is interrogated by a sphinx concerning just this question. Your survival depended on the right answer then and there. What mattered was the true lover's heart. The challenge is for you to answer — which you do, with a certain grace. The action comes from so high that it is impossible to respond in kind. This is the way the true philosopher faces death, the same for the true lover, who is the same. This is a literal death, death of death in the literal sense. Here you see the transmutation of base metal, that substance that consists in a transubstantiation of death. The base metal is indifference in the face of the riddle. It comes from the thought of death, not yet having been transmuted. Thought lacks animation and feels dead. If you can free yourself of it and its moribund quality, you can be alive at any moment. Whenever the true lover is alive, love is alive to the question. If it is not, the quest is dead in the sense of stillborn. It is simple to diagnose deadness. It stems from a lack of the desire to free yourself. Once desire comes, it comes from higher sources and seeks to return there. Desire is aim and purpose of your work. Without it, you will remain a dogmatist, cynic, or sophist, and listen exclusively to the negative sense of the word. When you have desire, you have a harmony of presence. Desire is none other than that, the fresh sparkle in what is presently provided. Desire that and you will succeed in life.

You could look to desire for being love as an answer, but it is not that. The enigma has no answer, right or wrong. You may think of the lover as having the right answer at just the right time, but that thought has been proven wrong. Orpheus, lover of presence, is the counterexample. Are you shocked to discover he has the wrong answer? It is obvious from the final outcome. The moment he turns to look for Eurydice is his greatest knowledge. Then he finds out how swiftly the sphinx intervenes, and there is death. The question remains a deadly enigma until someone gives the correct response. It may be news that there is one, but there is. The way to it involves what I came to call *bringing the third*. I will wait until the next chapter, how it alone respects the origin and destiny of the question. The origin is easy to say, since it is astral. It brings starry matter, material of an astral quality. The destiny is less clear to me. It has to do with a body of astral material that has a quality of the star realm. Your presence is also enlisted. Presence is the mother. She is wise and can provide the delicate, womb-like tissue in which a higher body may come to term.

Mothering may have been obvious to you since I spoke of the mother-liquor in the bath. Maternal presence is universal. It is water and earth. To an extent, air and fire enter into the maternal element. This aspect does not belong exclusively to the feminine side of humans. Mothering also is a quality of the androgyne who takes after its mother in this regard. For that is the sexual identity of your second body. It is a third or middle sex. Its desire is naturally to be loved. Since the androgyne embodies a memory of desire, it further assists transformation with an impulse to begin. Do not lose sight of how mothering is enigmatic in itself. The images can be looked at in this connection. It would be good to review them anyway. One says:

> *I bore the mother who gave me birth*
> *Through me she was born again upon earth.*

You can read the words in many ways, but for me they speak for the androgynous birth. They say how the mother is born again. This must refer to our higher identity, which is born through the mother. It matures from the conflict between affirming desires and denying ones. It results from a friction. From that, remembering rekindles though at first, it does not remember what. Gradually, the words recognize the embryo they bear within. An unborn life grows to be an over-riding consideration, more urgent than the other affairs of daily living. But do not believe this comes easy. Conscience is engendered by use of salt, as I said. Salt is the coin of what is important and using it makes sure words are not forgotten. I do not speak in terms of chronology, but I will say the astral body signifies a maturation of the process. Let it be your destiny, for its possession is substance of the stone.

There is another way to say what I mean. Think of how conscience carries an embryonic word of God. It wants you to read it. The book is a way of being true to its commandments. They are its flower to a nature true to itself. Do you doubt that the true lover is after anything other? That is why Socrates loves to emphasize how important conscience is, whenever Plato writes of his acting truly. I did not understand true action, but I feel at such moments, a new identity becomes incarnate. It is a 'condensation' of presence itself precipitating after distillation. It is the sac of waters that announces the end to the fetal life cycle and the start of birth. By analogy, imagine the second body is born after the waters of presence burst. This is long after the process when the second body becomes substantial. It is around the time wisdom is about to come into the world. It is about the time that conscience will welcome its beloved partner.

Were there prefigurations that we overlooked? Think back to when love began to search for a suitable vessel, and you see the need for great care. You don't want to repeat Psyche's mistake, when she scorches her beloved with the lamp she is searching with. Perhaps she lived too much in anticipation. Great care must be used in selecting a site. If you look at the teacher of conscience, the initial problem is a place for birthing. In the account, a manger in the barn, a shelter for animals, is the only shelter provided. There is hospitality there and nowhere else. If you think analogously, in the work of presence, the initial problem is the same. The second body is in need of a birthing place. It has been turned away from palace and mansion, inn and burgher's house. The place it eventually finds, its vessel, is correspondingly humble. It is a tomb—the tomb of its parents which is not exactly the most hospitable but exactly hospitable enough. You remember in passing how the second body first is a fine vapor that rises from intense energy of coupling. The intensity involves a war of desire against itself, bitterly divided, wanting mutual annihilation, and ending in an enigmatic death of both sides. The tomb lends its place, a quiet vault of silence, to the needs of the process. The enclosure hosts presence as it gathers itself in a labor. There, presence swells with child. You can see how the labor pains begin.

Can you say what is born? I ask you to avoid idle speculation and cut to the heart of the matter. You already know the birth we speak of is ongoing. It is incomplete, unfinished, and requiring more. It is not self-reliant or adequate to itself since we are imperfect beings that harbor some divisive thought or other. Besides, the process takes place in time and is in movement. If you try to grasp it, you will not succeed without sacrificing its life. You cannot put closure on it without yourself suffering seriously and becoming rigid in feeling. Desire means being in movement. Its motion is to circle around your center—the heart—every-ready to serve the center's desire. So you we must avoid thinking you have actually arrived there, or that there is such a thing as arriving at all. The thought that anything special will happen gives a wrong emphasis. What happens, happens 'over your left shoulder,' if you see what I mean. There, it will not cause a distraction. You need to allow experience to correspond to the flow. You must feel it to be ongoing, not stopping, never repeating, consistently with the new. At the same time, your experience cannot waste too much time with attention called to itself. A lighter attention lets you look more at reality. Do you see now that it is the seeing that comprises a new birth?

Love is always born love. Love is the subject of birth. Being born is the action of love, the subject. The circumstance is in this moment, or, you might say, the outcome of the flow. You must realize that the flow cannot really be seen but only contained momentarily in a vessel, the heart. There, enrapt, it will condense and take an androgynous form. We ourselves are two-thirds of the way blind. As limited as we are, we miss the overflowing font whose goodness fills the cauldron with the raw matter of a new life. What sense do you really have of the flow of which I speak? Do you see how it pours and from where it comes? I am referring to a subtle pressure that moves from in front of you to behind. If you lack the foggiest notion of the source, you will be handicapped. Be clear that by calling love the subject of birth, I am saying that love is doubly invisible. Love hides its advent. You will understand almost nothing of how birth takes place and even less of who is giving birth. You will know only that what is born is an exalted refinement of desire. 'Desire for love is no different from love itself.' This is both true and not true. Refined desire is no different yet altogether different from impulsive desire. This is the riddle of the drawings. In their circle, 1 to 9, love is not born until the ninth, but its astral configuration is there from the first. Now you can tell yourself that to be born, love needs a body. It must be on the earth but not of it. Love enters into duality and arrays itself in opposition, but never ceases to rise above them. Love's devotion must encompass the earth but never lose its allegiance to the astral realm.

THE TEACHER

We have a great hunger to learn from love's teacher. Don't you hunger to set your eyes on the one and bow? Don't you want to hear the voice and touch the body? Alas, this is your undoing. Your belief that the teacher is a real person or has a personal identity is costly. The teacher, to be sure, exists and is real. You have proof from the results of your encounter. Your search for love is aided at many points by the generosity of the teacher, most especially during the 'dark night' of desire. Then, when you call for help, it comes, but always unexpected and even unnoticed, save in retrospect. The teacher's reality, first and foremost, is hidden. It is the teacher's character to remain in the background, behind the curtain. We cannot point to one so quick. In a movement we students cannot follow, the teacher imparts a lesson in the course of things, then is gone. The trace, the golden script on the wall, is all we have. Yet it changes everything and we are gladdened by the memory of love. But nowhere in the event has the teacher made an appearance. Love's teacher wears a veil. We can assume that we are taught by a being from another order who is there at the right moment. We know no identity, even though we have had a direct encounter. Whenever we meet the teacher teaching, the teacher is looking the other way.

Orpheus' error lay in this direction. There is a great deal to be learned in his lesson. He sought the teacher face to face, the way you might encounter just anyone. When he turned to look, there was a figure receding, vanishing... nothing. As long as he walked with eyes averted, he showed respect for the teacher and the otherworldly station. This is absolutely essential because then he relied on a 'blindfold intuition' and received instructions 'by signs and miracles.' Orpheus' mistake was to want to put things into words and refuse the perception of his vessel. For the swiftness of the teacher and the delicate, subtle movement of intelligence defy the coarse, human way of feeling. In complete freedom, the teacher escapes the grasping desire that seeks to constrain rather than obey. The teacher offers gold. It gleams like starlight in our night vision.

It allures and entices, yet when you look directly, it is gone. Anything else is beside the point.

Psyche committed the same mistake. She sought the reassurance of sight to confirm the teacher's presence. Because of her greed, it was not enough to have experienced opening to love. She needed to face the source of its enigmatic work. As a result, love's teacher fled to beyond the pale until such a time when Psyche could prove herself through arduous trials. After that, she understood how the teacher works in reality. Teaching takes place but she cannot look, listen, or touch it. Light and sound cannot penetrate the source of it. Imagine that the teacher behaves like a cloud, a vaporous mass that the drawings depict. When you recognize this, you understand why the teacher lives in a cloud of unknowing.

Though you cannot meet love's teacher, its teaching is known through action. The act of teaching consists in *bringing the third*. The teacher brings the third and does nothing else. Can you see how bringing the third follows a secret path in life? When you receive it, you are on the path. It teaches to thoroughly mix positive and negative so that a new force of desire enters the world. The vessel is in us, at our center, the heart. Arnaut Daniel, the troubadour balladeer, sings of filling the vessel with the third. 'All that is,' he says, 'freezes, but I cannot be cold, for a new love makes my heart grow green again.' When your heart contains a simultaneous awareness of both the 'I want' and the 'I don't want,' there is a heat. Attracted to it, astral matter can find its way—like an electric current conducted by copper wire. The more durable substance slowly condenses to a second body. This body is dependent on the physical body the way an embryo is. The natal body is sustained by desire. It is well for you to mark the lesson, which is what I call bringing the third.

You could say that the teacher is the growing process itself. Bringing the third is the crux of the matter. From this, it follows that the third is brought by conscience since conscience alone is aware of the rightness of things. The essence of what the third brings is its right quality. It alone has the capability of nourishing the vessel's substance. Conscience is sensitive to a special quality that makes it an indispensable adjunct to the teacher. Conscience gives the teacher a voice you can recognize. But do not mistake what I say about conscience. It is not a monitor or policeman, but speaks to disseminate love's work. But it is not in itself wise either. Conscience is humble and receptive to the wisdom that love speaks. If you ask *what* is grown, the answer is a body. It is a living organization with higher faculties whose source is from above.

The coming of the third is illustrated by a special symbol. When it is brought, a 'holy rain' descends. It drops through the sky door and fills the volume of the physical body—concentrated in the heart and all the way to the skin, and beyond. Its finer matter can to penetrate the physical substance of the first body. Think of it as a body within a body. These bodies, however, are not nestled inside one another like kewpie dolls. The second occupies the same space as the first. But it can thoroughly blend with the first and not lose its own identity. Its frequency is higher, a resonance of where it came from. When it constitutes a new body, it incarnates an intelligence of the higher astral realm. When knowledge derives from that quickness, it is wise for it has no content. It expresses the perfect emptiness of the astral realm.

Bringing the third, one brings the wings of wisdom. Living wisdom, I must stress, is no delineation, archive, compendium, or encyclopedia. These are results culled from the forest. They are not living wisdom herself. Living wisdom flies aloft, above strife and duality. This is the meaning of the tenth *Rosarium* drawing. There, the androgyne hovers over the earth, the terrestrial realm of conflict. Its flight also suggests freedom. Wisdom is for free and costs nothing, but only after you pay the price. Wages vary, as the parable of the vineyard tells, but wisdom is freedom. Being free, the special intelligence soars where it wishes, desirous to return to origin. Yet it is still bound to earth and when it soars too far, the fool brings it back. The fool remembers how to trip anyone up, even a sage, and so brings you down to earth. The fool once used wings, like wisdom's, but now prefers to bring the third in his own fashion. His irony derides pretension in favor of wisdom. His big discovery is fool's gold. He reminds you of it constantly, and for this alone, wisdom rewards the fool with love.

Wisdom has a short life and lives in the moment. It invites you to do the same. The evasion of your duty means that you do not bring the third, but only the first or second. One brings conflict and two brings struggle. The life that the third brings has nothing to do with conflict, struggle, disagreement or disharmony. Wisdom simply animates and balances the forces of life. The wise one keeps a low center of gravity, like a turtle. Follow the animation and you grow quiet and empty. Just here is where to find two essential properties of wisdom. Since wisdom does not contain anything, it holds nothing back. It is absolutely free from any desire to become a vessel, and so is the perfect substance for a vessel to desire to contain. It flows perfectly and overflows any heart desirous of it.

You may deduce that wisdom sets a light out but does nothing more. When the third is brought, it changes nothing. It neither adds nor subtracts from what is provided. What is providential suffices because wisdom makes due with it superlatively. Its abundance lets wisdom be free of providence because it depends only on itself. Wisdom is what providence provides for, and in the spirit of wisdom, does so with plenty. A measure of its plenitude is how wisdom constantly outgrows its own skin. When the third is brought, with wisdom, the lover only then becomes visible. Before the third is brought, the lover waits in obscurity, unsure of the source of its provisions. The view is beclouded, as the drawing proclaims. Meaning is clouded, but when the cloud evaporates, the meaning of the third turns out to be deeply enigmatic. Who does the androgyne represent? The enigma is no disturbance in our perception, but an essential characteristic of the third. The third stirs up your questions. What is it? What does it want? Where does it come from? What is it for? The questions remain.

Enigma is the way the third's otherworldly origin. Its aura of paradox was prefigured by the stranger who is cloaked as a foreigner who comes to be loved. The stranger unleashes an attraction from which pure essence of love will flow—but not until a series of procedures work and refine the crude desire. The third must be brought at a number of junctures. If not, the process gets only so far before collapsing to unrefined ore. The way that stranger comes from elsewhere suggests the mysterious third. An outsider, the stranger possesses qualities to shock you. You are lover and thus the stranger brings what can be loved—the third. The third is in the nature of a shock and in any shock to the awareness, the third is brought. You must know how all such shocks come from above, in contrast to how shocks from below cause only additional conflict and threaten our equilibrium. They leave you tense and closed. In each shock, if you look closely, there is a flicker of the lustrous light of stars. Look quickly, since it is mercurial and loves to hide.

Although in itself incomprehensible, you need to understand that the third is not given. This is one of the most ancient insights into reality. Do you grasp its meaning? What is not given must be brought. Bringing is the opposite of giving. If no one will give you wine, you must bring it along. Yet the third certainly is nothing you can carry. Just the reverse. It is far too light, fickle, and changeable for that. Highly perishable, it has a life that must be renewed at each breath. Otherwise, it gets stale and molded. It may be obvious to you that I am speaking of the impulse to begin. That is what you are responsible for bringing. Then, the enigmatic third isn't far behind. Think of the third as an invisible theater in which beginnings play. The curtain rises, there is action, and we are part of the audience in the theater of the third. Remember, you are in a theater of great antiquity. It is primordial in purpose and exists for birthing. With each beginning act, it gives birth to life's new drama. 'In each beginning is my end' is the language of the third. In the end, Hamlet cries, 'But I do prophesy the election lights/On Fortinbras, he has my dying voice.' He is aware of how another order is about to arise out of the old. The third, invisible, imperturbable, will usher in it. It will survive with new life to replace Hamlet's passing and all that is passing with him.

You cannot directly bring the third, but nonetheless, must bring it. It is the challenge of your destiny, to make the golden birth. By now, you know how in the conjunction and destruction of the first and second, death has a special attribute. It is a conscious death that concerns our science. The entire underworld journey moves from consciousness to greater consciousness. The third initially appears like a vapor rising, a strange, metallic vapor. It promises to bring a fertile rain but hasn't yet. The cloud has not yet stabilized but has properties of the third: it is durable, indestructible, and fresh. Its appearance may be fleeting, but it leaves an indelible mark on you. You are not the same person as the one who heretofore has been unable to bring the enigma to bear on the process. Now you are an alchemist!

You are to be marked as among the true lovers. This is the special discipline in which I initiate you. They, like the true philosophers, reject the adversity of dualism. They no longer are attracted by conflict, contradiction, and their ideologies. What then is their belief? They are the strange ones because they adhere to nothing. They are versatile and fluent in every word they say but live only for one love—a vision of the beloved. It alone is truth, the quicksilver. Evanescent and effervescent, pouring from above, it runs like water through the fingers and moistens each thought and feeling with its 'dew.' To hold it is an impossible feat. A characteristic sensation of wetness gives a confirmation of the teacher's proximity. When you feel the fluid flux, the teacher is in the vicinity. You can then expect to grow animated and eager to learn, if somewhat nervous. But that is not all. The whole entourage I have been introducing to you will be there. Alongside the teacher, the fool dances and gives a running account of your shortcomings as a lover so as to enlighten your self-esteem and vanity. Beloved truth is at times giddy with foolishness and always thin and ragged from constantly moving about. You will see what I speak of when you behold the one truth whose sight true lovers love to see. Then you will see it is not different from the love their sight sees. They are twin aspects of the androgyne who is the incarnation of the third. They are disguised, of course, you already you have glimpsed them out of concealment. They are lover and beloved.

Do you think that the expression, *bringing the third,* is simply a logical one? It is more illogical than that if you mean for logic to keep your thinking straight. The teacher relies on means that are bent, as truth or the pathway of love is. If thought could set things right, there would be no need for the arcane sciences. But need there is and it is enormous. Therefore, you should realize that what I call the third, which is to say spirit or the Holy Ghost, comes and goes on its own. It obeys no logic, human or inhuman. No one can say where the wind listeth. If the task is to bring the third, it might seem like bringing the ocean in a leaky bucket, or what stories speak of. Does Psyche not have to bring a vial of Persephone's beauty to pass Aphrodite's test? Does Gilgamesh try to bring back the plant of immortality? Look upon the task in this way. An opportunity presents itself. It has been provided and came to pass. Then, if you can, you are witness to how the third, that no one else could bring, has brought itself. It happens at the point that logic breaks down, when contraries do their arabesque. Peace from the near side of struggle comes to roost under the new order. This is the time when, in fairy tales, the youngest son, long since given up for dead, returns with a cure for his father's terminal illness. From nowhere, from foreign land, in the guise of one back from the dead, he has brought the third. It is an act that simply is not repeatable. But then again, he will never have to do it again.

If you are acquainted with these illogicalities, you will know better what to expect. If you do not, there is the lesson of Orpheus. He followed the natural urge to know love's teacher face to face, and it was his undoing. Can he teach you? We want our relations with the third to be logical. In our thinking, we suppose a recipe exists for bringing the third. Can you see now how belief in a formula is fallacious? The art involved is more an improvisation than a scripted reading. I do not mean it is abracadabra, but there is a special spell to let things happen. All this implies that you will recognize the teacher's presence only out of the corner of your eye, just out of reach. It is quicker than thought and already gone before being brought. So do not repeat Orpheus' mistake. Remember what is up to you, an initiative. Love's teacher will come when you are unaware and will act so discreetly that you will see only in retrospect. Patience is a necessity but it also is a gift. Nonetheless, you must learn to wait until you find the wherewithal to bring the third. The great circle of love will remain sealed, and you outside, until that one small movement is remembered. Until then, you will find not a single drop of life, even though your vessel bobs on the infinite suffering ocean.

A faceless teacher with no name teaches love of life—a lesson that cannot be taught. The less you are bothered by paradox and the less confused by a missing identity, the more you can summon the wherewithal to bring the third. You are dealing with the question of transmutation and it does not concern itself with who the teacher is. Those terms apply to the realm of impulsive desire, but not to its newly refined form. The teacher teaches that same mystery that we learn through the hard road of desire: the love to be loved. It is the only road that teaches and the only one on which you meet one who knows love's teaching. You are on it because you are lacking in love, in the infinity that love promises. The lack will draw the teacher to you, much as man attracts woman and woman man. The teacher will be drawn but you will not see who comes. Only afterwards will you feel the mystery of sudden rapture, the full release of finally being loved by the beloved.

I would ask you to go gently into this night. The teaching seeks no direct confrontation with love. Love, its teacher and its blessing, is not a well-met-fair-chap occasion. That would be if it were it a crude matter of control. Love that is managed, manipulated, or adulterated is not the love that is the distillation of desire. Love is not subject to domination because there is no subject of love. There is no one who bears love like a predicate unless it be the lover. The lover has devised a vessel in which to keep love's most volatile substance. The lover keeps what cannot be kept just as the lover loves one immeasurably more loving. This means that the lover is the receptive one and has no authority to issue commands. The author of love, the beloved, comes and goes as she will. Her unbounded willingness means that she is eager for an invitation. But because she is contained by no one, whoever takes her in possesses no one and is not the subject of a possession. If you follow my thinking, you find that she cannot be encountered through the front door. As I said, you need to learn about the sky door that opens to the rain flowing down from the ether. It comes to vivify you. That alone teaches a full love of life since you drink from the fount and imbibe its infinitely restorative power.

At the fountain, you will find that it is impossible not to experience the impulse to begin. It rains from above as you get near. The philosopher can say how love enters at the beginning, if it enters at all. Philosophy can tell how, even before the process, it already is pure, but exceedingly limited in quantity. The moment you grasp that, you feel the need for more. This is no greed but an honest hunger for value. How can there be more? Later, you see that raw material is everywhere, though not pure, still only an ore. It exists to be refined if the lover's desire to be whetted. The desire is very real, is reality itself. For the task you will outfit yourself in the gold of initiative. Otherwise, desire is in mortal danger of going unaddressed. Without gold, your desire for love will be frustrated by its own lack and you will suffer blindly. These pangs of conflict you already know well, so mark them. Better to suffer love wisely, for then you join in with the great work that I am schooling you for. Better to drink deeply and feel the thirst, unslaked, ever-parching, so that you may learn the precious metal of which you are made.

Now you are ready to know a latter step. Give up distinguishing love from desire and learn to love with love's eyes. The lover feels desire flash in the course of a day. Each flash is Heraclitus' fire. Beauty flaming from the word has the power to put each thing in its rightful place. Each comes to life and shows the illumined face of life. Saying 'life' I mean love, for by now you surely recognize their near kinship. They are twins, red and white, Esau and Jacob, gripping the other's ankle. Or they seem to be, though the same fire resides in the alchemist's furnace. See it reflected on your own face, as it is from the true philosopher's. The force of love and life is one and the same, beauty. Beauty attracts and suddenly you wake. Beauty leaves a trace in each thing and you wake to a need for transcendence. Flashes of desire wake you to a possible elsewhere. They are ciphers of a more luminous light, more divine yet more human. They speak of a perfect life whose overtones whisper on every level. Each is charged with enigmatic significance. Each whispers the truth that the lover longs to hear.

I have told you about the descending force of the fount. Its action originates above the plane of duality. It is a measure of freedom and freely enters the place of war and conflict. Above all, it brings peace. It unites disunited, disheartened things. It heals division and divided allegiances. If you invite it, it will come. The force loves to be where you desire it to be. As you have learned, where attraction exists, love comes to stay, if only for blink of an eye. That radically changes how things become. Life as a whole deepens and grows increasingly desirous. To that intensity that love is called, and you will come to call love that same intensity. From the nourishment of your desire, love's body swells and thickens and its life grows in strength and clarity. So does your desire because it listens to what comes from the heart. Your heart remembers its experience of listening to stone. There, in the silent tomb, the lover listened. The lover still does. The lover, with absolute mineral nature, it hears and learns as much as the philosopher. The philosopher hears the absolute absence of anything to be heard. Is this not the secret teaching of death? At least, I assume this is how Socrates must have spoken to his pupils. He told us, when he was at death's gate, to look across and to 'sacrifice a cock to Aesculapius.' So the philosopher reminds us how life comes to the dead.

I do not wish to make it sound easy. Mostly, you will object to opposition and disharmony, and that makes for difficulty. We live constantly with the objection, knowingly or not. It is our shadow. The more you get to know it, the more you will see the main obstacle. Impulse desires to get relief from suffering disharmony. But it is not an intelligent approach, soothing disagreement by dulling memory. Something else is needed. To start, you need a thirst, since a thirst for love is what invites the teacher. How the thirst comes is as enigmatical as its inability to be slaked. The miracle lies in a reversal that comes in acceptance of your finitude. Then there is satisfaction in inadequacy, knowledge in imperfection. You might turn to the teacher of conscience, Jesus, for a clue about what a satisfying taste might consist in. Being satisfied by an unappeasable desire for love is what it feels like under the fountain of life. He speaks the words of the fountain when he says, 'Whoever drinks from my mouth will become like me.'

EPILOGUE

Orpheus, I told you, is no ordinary being but a hero of presence. He keeps guard over the impulse to begin. As he walks up the hill from hell's gate, he carries the memory of his impossible task. At the fringe of awareness, the terrible cost lingers of forgetting one small moment. You find him holding distraction at arm's length, vigilant, and observant. The strength required is superhuman. He manages to summon it until . . .

Until his amnesia, Orpheus remains a lover. He is a lover of the first rank, drinking in the down-pouring of above. You might imagine him walking mouth agape in the rain, continually vivified in his effort. As he keeps guard against a wandering thought, he takes on the role of host. He keeps the door open to the unexpected, since things seem attractive to a lover's heart when sustained by its beloved. Look at Orpheus more closely. He is human, in many ways like yourself. He possesses a certain wisdom, seasoned with a little foolishness. You find this out when he strings his lyre and lets the song get the better of him. He is not naïve. He is saved from that by an accumulation of astral matter. He has paid for it through the same transaction I have urged on you. You can see how he intuits something of the ethereal and starry realm, as well as beyond it. His memory of obligation is sustained by a sensation that the cosmos itself requires the duty of him. But then, in one instant, all that changes. Orpheus spills his vial of quicksilver. He forgets.

That lapse does not degrade him. Perhaps it even elevates his accomplishment, or at least brings it into your view. Even after he forgets, Orpheus remains an absolute lover. He has been marked. The story goes on. There is deep sorrow, but it passes. As lover, he cannot bemoan fate for long. It is what was provided, and he, keeper of presence, must not lose track. The object of his true love is gone. Eurydice has been whisked away to the halls of the dead forever. Now his song is a call to her in her absence. Elegiac, lamenting, it sings now of the absented true love. This is where Orpheus' genius rises to new heights. The song makes Eurydice's absence equivalent to her presence. Overjoyed, Orpheus again wakes the impulse to begin. It is different for him now, having passed through the salt of remorse. Now he can begin with harmony.

Reconciled to adversity, he conveys presence with far greater authority. Will the underworld gods take pity on him a second time?

In reality, that his beloved is gone forever he cannot believe. You see how he looks everywhere for her, keeping himself attentive. Great nature weeps with his sorrow but cannot change his fate. Gradually, his grief seeps into his very cells and transforms him. It awakens him and he feels what he must himself do. Consciously he dies to himself in a forlorn, forgotten place. His intention calls a feminine rage from within the earth, and the Maenads appear. They tear his body limb from limb. The head they hurl into the Aegean Sea. The mouth continues with its immortal song. The song sings and prophesies of love's transmutation. It tells how to achieve the incorruptible stone.

The rendering of the story, which I bequeath to you, has been an Orphic exercise. Do you understand what the stone of memory consists in? What is the stone? It is for that—and not Eurydice—that Orpheus submitted to the underworld. He went there for a memory that had been inscribed on a clay tablet. That tablet tells of initiation into the impulse to begin. It is the dowry of his bride Eurydice. The stone of memory, that most precious, was in his possession, but he let go. Now he must find it.

Because song overflows from his mouth, you need to see that Orpheus also is the teacher. He brings love's teaching. But you must be clear about how the loss of his beloved Eurydice plays its part. In the tragedy of a momentary, involuntary lapse, Orpheus meets his dread. It is the exact opposite of his strongest desire. The collision of the two causes a death in him that transforms his heart. Before, he took his task to remember presence and took it most seriously. Now, he is able to forget presence because he *is* it. His obligation is fulfilled and gratitude overflows from him. He passes over to the truth as soon as death is met and duty accomplished. Do you understand his accomplishment? The greatness of Orpheus? The mystery of conjunction is death. The mystery always is death. That mystery draws you to question life and search for the incorruptible stone, your destiny. Death completes a circle and frees you to . . . life. As you go, you gather material and become the mystery of stone. Orpheus encircles the mystery and becomes eternal song. As long as his song plays on, he lives. Do you see how this is so?

Orpheus may be a teacher, but you can see no path he teaches. Look as you might, there is no clue. It takes a while to grasp, but as Orpheus passes onward, he leaves no trace. There are countless songs of Orpheus, ancient ones, modern ones. These are songs of great depth and beauty but give no indication of how he went about his discoveries. They cannot. The path of Orpheus is a traceless one. He is a teacher of a path that cannot be traced. He teaches it well, for many people have followed. I may claim myself to be one, but it takes a more patient ear than I have to listen.

The conscious death and journey through the underworld that I led you through is a preparation. It is a cleansing, purging, and refining phase. What the tomb ultimately purifies is the nothingness of death. For death is nothing, an immense emptiness behind everything. It is a backdrop where there is no thing. To recognize its presence to life sweeps the surface clean down to essence. Orpheus teaches it by how he walks and by the sound he makes. Nature responds, often in ways unknown to reason. He teaches of a nothing that contains everything and is in everything, but leaves no mark. Orpheus is a teacher of the ether.

This region is where the other dwells. It is also known as the mother-region because it is a container of life in that it supports it invisibly and yet is not life. Am I not talking about the vessel? The vessel, therefore, is undying and eternal. These are properties of the ether. It is so infinitely permeable that no substance can, for an instant, impede its flow. Nonetheless, it is a flask like a plasma container. If you can follow my thinking, you see that I am talking about the nothingness of God, the Absolute.

The nothingness is not so immense that it doesn't enter our world, this earth. Isn't that what Orpheus teaches, if only you would follow. He shows you how the nothingness exists before your unseeing eyes and unhearing ears. It is from where, at that most holy point, the fount overflows. Nothingness holds the origin of things. This is what I mean by saying the womb is to be found in the tomb. In the tomb, you learn about a simultaneous awareness of life and its opposite—the ultimate duality, from which the rest falls. There, you glimpse what neither lives nor dies but is incorruptible and ever-fresh. Orpheus would relay knowledge of the singularity which is the impulse to begin. For this reason, know him as the teacher of the stone.

Most eloquent of beings, he sings and sings endlessly of it. Perhaps he is most fluent in the mode of lamentation, like Jeremiah. Then, he brings tears that melt like wax in the fire of his heart. But do not think him a messenger of sorrow. There is music other than the lament. Odes, prophecies, spells, blessings, prayers: there are many strings in his lyre. Although he sings under the star-filled sky, of what he sings, he never reveals. This is because the beloved of his song may only be evoked. He can do nothing to disclose the path to her on because it is pathless and can be uncovered only one step at a time. He lives with this rigor and nevertheless sings—never an idle song but sings of strength, endurance, and will. You could put the matter like this: where he stands is immaterial as long as you know he sings of a great mystery. To it, we wake. Orpheus is a teacher who wakes us.

In our deep disharmony, his song sounds an alarm. It shocks like unearthly beauty can, shattering the dream of existence. I would only say how profoundly it disturbs me to catch its refrain and find my gaze going from my heart, skyward to the distant stars. That is its condition. Its beauty has the further virtue of 'sweetening the bitter.' Orpheus sings and I wake to my parched state. I feel shame and suffering. Then, I listen as though water is being poured into a thirsty mouth. Life returns then, but not the same life I have just left. It is a gift but you must understand how he is in no position to give gifts. He is no god, but gains immortality by the same means open to us. He partakes of the ether. Orpheus sings of filling the astral body and that is what he teaches. He teaches the laws of growth of our incorruptible, never dying body. As he wanders across the face of the earth, Orpheus leaves no trace. He has no followers for what is there to follow? The sole trace of Orpheus is left in the stars, a pale light that meanders across the Milky Way. You will need to locate it before you can truly begin.

He takes our disharmony in stride and through his song uncovers its hidden harmony. In this regard, he is master of bringing the third, the mark of an authentic teacher, who has passed the 'tests' and is self-certified. Do not think you will ever lay eyes on Orpheus! I did for many years, but now know better. You will sense how the teacher comes by, dispensing the third, solely by a unique wakefulness. Body, mind, and heart then share an awareness of love's miracle. Nonetheless, whatever way you look, there will be no sign of the teacher. He has vanished without a trace. You will be left with a memory as fluid as quicksilver, fluent as Orpheus' songs, and quick as his message. That memory contains a seed of presence. Because its purpose has not yet burgeoned forth, there are questions. Are these true signs? What do they mean? How are you supposed to be? This is how to learn the suppleness of his music.

Orpheus' is consumed by his vocation. As he walks along the traceless way, the songs emerge as traces of the untraceable road to the stars. Whoever you meet on it has an incorruptible body. They, like you, have ceased pretending and seek a far more serious and courageous goal. It requires a large dash of sacrifice. Orpheus has practiced the science I am describing to you and has come to believe in its efficacy—not like the incredulous, but as one who has tested himself. In the stories, Orpheus inherits the lyre that Hermes invented for Apollo. It is made of a tortoise shell. Its mineral composition is that of the stone. When Orpheus plays it, the melody is the stone's elemental faith, the source of faith itself. His songs turn the heart toward the grain of that substance so that the ear can better listen. The stars own their own intrinsic melody and it is echoed by his knowing fingers. The music overflows and moves in the direction of the traceless. His faith is a finger pointing to that.

In the ancient accounts, the decapitated head of Orpheus continued to sing as it floated out on the Adriatic Sea. I imagine it somewhere still, a knot of seaweed for a disguise. The mouth has lost none of its perfect pitch. No one will ever find the source of its music though lightened we continue to be by its eternal sound.

AFTERWORD

Thus ends the manuscript of *The Shock of Love*, or more exactly, my reconstruction of it. It is now some years after the completion of my work and still more since the original discovery of the manuscript. The questions surrounding it have, if anything, sharpened. I feel something of the plight of the legendary border guard who caught the arm of Lao Tzu as he was passing outside into the wild, sat him down, and had him write down the *Tao*. That man must have anguished over his act, whether it was to bring a blessing to humankind, or a curse—or both. I sometimes find solace in imaging Paolo, secure in his retirement to a Provencal or Adriatic fishing village, or in some lower heaven. Would not that ironic smile be on his lips at the sight of our attempt to make scholarly good sense of the puzzle? And yet, would our effort, feeble or misguided as it is, not also tickle him? Paolo was a lover. Like his divine counterpart, Orpheus, his singing on immortally resonates to reveal all things, for better and for worse. His challenge lies in locating the equanimity of mind that marks acceptance, both of truth and of untruth. It is this great comfort in the midst of discomfort that is his signature of the project.

About the Author

David Appelbaum lives in the Shawangunk Mountains of New York State. He is a student of esoteric philosophy.

ALL THINGS THAT MATTER PRESS ™

FOR MORE INFORMATION ON TITLES AVAILABLE FROM
ALL THINGS THAT MATTER PRESS, GO TO
http://allthingsthatmatterpress.com
or contact us at
allthingsthatmatterpress@gmail.com